BoneWalker

BONEWALKER

a novel

KAREN LEE WHITE

EXILE
editions

singular fiction, poetry, nonfiction, translation, drama, and graphic books

Library and Archives Canada Cataloguing in Publication

Title: Bonewalker / Karen Lee White.

Names: White, Karen Lee, 1956- author.

Identifiers: Canadiana (print) 20230560113 | Canadiana (ebook) 20230560121 |
  ISBN 9781990773228 (softcover) | ISBN 9781990773235 (EPUB) |
  ISBN 9781990773242 (Kindle) | ISBN 9781990773259 (PDF)

Subjects: LCGFT: Novels.

Classification: LCC PS8645.H5425 B66 2024 | DDC C813/.6 — dc23

Copyright © Karen Lee White, 2023
Book and cover designed by Michael Callaghan
Cover and Endpapers paintings by Mark Preston
Typeset in Garamond font at Moons of Jupiter Studios
Published by Exile Editions Ltd ~ www.ExileEditions.com
  144483 Southgate Road 14, Holstein, Ontario, N0G 2A0
Printed and bound in Canada by Gauvin

We gratefully acknowledge the Government of Canada and Ontario Creates for
their financial support toward our publishing activities.

Canadian sales representation:
The Canadian Manda Group, 664 Annette Street, Toronto ON M6S 2C8
www.mandagroup.com 416 516 0911

North American and international distribution, and U.S. sales:
Independent Publishers Group, 814 North Franklin Street,
Chicago IL 60610 www.ipgbook.com toll free: 1 800 888 4741

For my mother Joan Rosemary Playfair (nee White),
who taught me to see beauty everywhere.

BONEWALKER

Like a fish released from the sea that was your Mother's womb, your tiny chest rises and falls, rises and falls, rises and falls. How does it know to do that?

Your name is "Stands in the Middle."

You who were handed down from above will know the two worlds, stand between the two worlds, live between the two worlds.

We are born holding all knowledge. As you grow, your duty is to remember it. There are things that live in darkness and must be illumined by the light.

Born a warrior; you will find and stand in the balance of honour and dishonour. You will not fear the exquisite nor the vile. This I will teach you. You and I are one with that space between; this is our curse and our blessing.

You and I, our Grandmothers and Grandfathers dream one another in the space between; between sleep and awakening, between worlds, between earth and sky. We can all meet there, but first, it must be in dreams.

They once showed me how they see us in our living world. Stars shining below from earth to sky. Looking together; from the above to beneath, through the black, on these below stars that were you, and I.

They come together tonight, our Old Ones, in the space between. In ancient regalia, the finest quillwork, smoky brain tanned fringed hide, woven cedar bark, made soft for wearing; a story belt here and wampum there.

Our Grandfathers will brew campfire tea. This is to greet you, their new child. In the in-between, it is not the women but the men who bring the water, start the fire to make medicine to share. Labrador tea, spruce tea, sage tea, nettle tea, pine tip tea, all were harvested and carried to the meeting place by each.

If we could see them now, they would move through coloured light, shimmer like the gossamer rainbow in the sun wing flash of a dragonfly. We could hear these colours between beats of a hummingbird's wing if you and I would ever learn to listen.

They use spirit names; earth names are not remembered here. Our old relations from before speaking in a gentle tone, a language they all understand. If we hear, it is a music redolent of peace. I have heard it in dreams. They speak in music words now of what you and I will need to know.

Each of our old relations will travel to us as we sleep. They will whisper, "You are warriors of a new age; live a new ceremony; speak your prayers to the tree of life."

They intone tearfully and say,

"Be courageous; help us. Heal the people." They sing these words in our ears at night; we understand these olden voices redolent of love.

Deep within a knowing those Old Ones wish us to free the people from chaos, pain, the darkness.

Our response is the oath we write with our heart's blood, an embrace from us to them; our great love (theirs the heart, ours the blood that moves through) reaching back to the space within we all hold between earth and sky.

◉◉◉

I'm going to tell this story the way you butcher a moose. Bleed it out; spill the guts of it right on the ground. It's the only way to tell it. All the funk of a warm, opened, wild animal will hit you right where you stand.

I'm not saying this is an easy one to tell. It's going to be me bleeding and gut spilling. But here goes.

Ever notice, that from the air, roads are pretty at much at angles and rivers snake? From the ground, you don't have the same perspective.

My life was a snaking river. I never knew which way it was going to turn. The only thing I knew for sure is that the river would keep on moving. There is a lie I have been carrying all my life. The lie is that I killed someone. Someone who did not deserve to die. I didn't kill her outright; I just stood by as she died a little at a time. Each time someone beat her, swore at her, demoralized her butterfly spirit, I did nothing. Was silent. When she was tormented, abused, kidnapped, held at gun-point, shot at, choked and brutalized, I stood by, heartless. Detached. I witnessed it all. That person I killed? It was me.

He was taken in the time of wild roses. Their scent everywhere, released into the breeze most potently at dawn and dusk, an ever-present reminder of her cavernous and unendurable loss. The evocation of roses, which she had once loved terribly, makes her ill. She loathes the look of them, their frail beauty evokes a volcanic rage. How can something beautiful exist in this ugly world? She uproots, hacks them out of her backyard, but they come back filled with hope. They tear her flesh, she curses, but each time a resilient shoot appears she destroys any sign of them. They always return. They hold the most delicate of blossoms, they are easily destroyed by wind, rain.

Their vines and petals are strong healing medicine. Their fruit is a medicine tea.

She imagines her heart as a war-bombed basement, nothing but devastation.

She knows he was worth living for, trying for, sacrificing for. A sweet child of seven; filled with the joy of discovery and already touched by the harshness of life. Each laugh was a gift to her. Each smile was a balm to her own long suffering. The loss of him was almost too great to bear.

June 16, 2000
Dearest Krie,

I am packing up your toys. It feels wrong to do this. I somehow think that if I leave your things out, you will be back for them. It has been eight months, and the counsellor tells me it is time to accept what is. How can I? I don't know where you are or what has happened. I don't know if you are safe, or your life has been taken. Not knowing is the worst. It's like a hulking monster in my closet. It never leaves. I try to remember how you laughed, the warmth of your little body as you hugged me tightly on your way by to run out the door to play. I don't allow myself to cry for you, I don't allow myself to feel the pain of losing you. [She takes a knife, cuts her hand, and watches as her blood drip, drip, drips to the page.]

Somehow, somewhere, your DNA exists. If your life was taken, still it exists. I see this blood of mine on this paper, and it links me to where you are, even if I don't know, because I bandaged your bleeding knees, cleaned your scratches. I still have your hair from your brush. It smells like you. I see you each day that I wake. I get up thinking that I need to get your breakfast, to get you up for school. Then I remember. This is a waking nightmare. Some

4

mornings, my first thought is "Oh yes, he is gone." It is in those moments that it's hard to catch my breath, and the pain in my chest feels as though a large bear has my heart in its paws and is squeezing the life out of me.

I do not know how to hold hope. I do not know how not to. I don't know how to grieve your loss. The only truth is that you are gone. Who took you – and where? My worst fear is that I do know, but do not allow myself to think of it, it is too horrible. I will live those first moments for the rest of my life. When I came out of the kitchen to call you for lunch, you were out of sight. Right then, in that beat of my heart, I knew. That second my heart stopped. Then it dropped straight to my feet. At that moment, the pain moved into my being and has made a home. We are not friends but are accustomed to one another. The pain is the parasite, I am the host. We need each other to survive.

Truthfully, I left with you, and I don't know where I have gone either. [She puts the pen down; she cannot write more.]

She feels only rage and tearing grief. One day she walks through the grocery store, pushing her cart, silent tears flowing down a stone face. She does not care. She cannot. At home, she smashes things to pieces and is furious that she must replace them. The young people at the mobile store look at her strangely. Except for the young Native boy who works there; he grins like a kid when she enters.

"Hi, Auntie, how are you today?"

"I'd better not answer that, my boy."

"One day it will be better."

"Only if he comes home."

"Only now you need a new phone, right, Auntie?"

She looks at him with a "What do you think?" expression.

"Try this one, Auntie, only this time we add the Otter case, so you can throw it like it's a spear."

He makes her smile a little but that hurts, too.

The agony of her heart sometimes wanes into numbness. It's not stillness, just a strange white place of no feeling. She does not know what she hates more – the agony or not feeling. One day she puts on a pair of shoes she has not worn for almost a year. She feels a sharp jab. She reaches down and finds a piece of LEGO. This was the child's game, from when he could crawl. To hide a LEGO piece in her shoe. She sits down on the floor and releases a howl. It transforms to keening, crying, screams. It is the sound of a wild animal. She does not feel better. The terrible sound only tells her that within there is a huge gaping, bleeding wound that cannot possibly heal.

She goes through the motions of living – eats, bathes, cleans, drives, breathes, moves – without thought, robotic. Nothing matters. It is down to what is necessary. She imagines that this is how animals in the wild must live. Responding to the need to eat, to sleep, to urinate, defecate, to clean, to fight, to survive. She does not fight or survive; she simply continues.

The small boy is in darkness. Cannot move. Confusion, then fear steals over him like cold air. The fear floods and contains him more than the darkness. Is he dead? Georgie says that when you die there is nothing but darkness. It squeezes his heart and feels like a cold wet fog on his skin. It hurts his chest. Dying, he thinks, would be like floating in darkness. He is not floating. He feels something digging into his back. He smells gasoline. He is trembling from cold. He tastes his own tears.

He hopes he is alive. Wherever he is, he does not want to be here.

Like a coyote, the man catches the scent of fear and a boy who has shit his pants. Damn, he thinks. Why had he not planned for this?

His new child is not going to be like the last one who died. He hadn't planned that either. When he had reached his remote cabin and opened the trunk, he found a still child. Pale blue, cold, dead. Having forgotten to ensure adequate air to the trunk of the car, when he removed the gag, he found the boy had suffocated. He remembers the blind panic like it was a day ago. It had taken him some time to decide. He had buried the child up high in the alpine. It had been a hard hike up, but he had wanted to place him where he would never be found. Where the air was clean and still. In a place where there were few animals to disturb the tiny body. He had placed a marker, a pile of rocks, where he could come sometimes. Something went quiet in him that day, as quiet as the dead boy.

Mother dreams of her child waving at her from a boat on a lake. Filled with joy she calls to him. She feels a presence, turns and sees a man bent with suffering. She knows this man. She cannot remember his name now that she is desperate to call out to him. He wades out to the boy, gets in the boat, and rows the boat away. She is left crying on the cold beach. Why did they not take her? Why did the boy not call out for her? Why did he let the man row him away from her?

She wakes with the pillow soaked with tears; tears still cool on her face. Switches on a light, finds her slippers and robe. She is impatient with bodily sensations such as cold; it removes her from her grief. She feels guilty to be distracted from it. She writes:

Son, I dreamt of you. You were with a man I know but cannot remember who he is now that I am awake. You went with him and did not call out to me. [Tears splash beside the blood spatters on the page, between her words.]

What I am to do? I cry harder with each of your toys I place in this bin in which this letter will wait for you.

I miss the smell of the outside on your hair. I miss your laugh coming down the hall from where you play in the bath. I miss the water you leave on the floor. I miss you kicking me awake at night. I miss cleaning your pee around the toilet and am sorry I got after you about that all the time. I miss movie night, and I miss hearing you come in the door. I even miss tripping over your shoes. I miss having to hang up your jacket from where you dropped it on the floor. I miss making your lunch. I miss dropping you at school and seeing and hearing all your friends call your name. I miss the little pictures you drew me. I miss you telling me about your dreams.

I am not a good Mother. I did not protect you. You are gone, and I should know where you are. A good Mother would know, would follow you like a wolf sniffing the ground, and catch your scent. Find you. Never let you go.

☉☉☉

The child holds on to a memory, where he speaks quietly playing with his trucks and army men, out by the big tree. He should have told Mother.

His Saturday morning happiness is shadowed by a dark sense. The hair on his back, neck, scalp rises, quivers. The feeling blocks the light of the autumn sun as if he has taken the first plunge into cold lake water.

He is not afraid. He knows this sensation, though has no actual memory of it. He knows to pretend that he needs to go into the house. He breathes, feeling that breath move in and out, as he takes the breeze within his lungs. He lines up his trucks. He knows not to run. Instead, rises slowly, looks at the sun, and brushes dirt, sticks and leaves off his knees. Stretches. Picks up his jacket where it lays crumpled. Shakes it. Throws it coolly over his shoulder. He feels the quickening of his heart, hears the steps behind him. He knows to show no sign of fear. He walks deliberately and slowly through the back door, kicks off his boots, hangs up his jacket. Only then does he wheel to face the predator. He sees nothing, but he knows it hunkers in the doorway. The chill in his stomach is as though he is standing up to his belly in a lake with a stiff breeze raising the bumps on his skin when the water feels warmer than the wind.

"You don't frighten me. *GAGEEAMAH*!"

He yells these last words, and Mother turns from the sink, half smiling, half frowning.

"Goodness, my boy, who on earth are you yelling at?"

"Nobody," he says firmly, resolute. "Nothing," he adds with a hint of anger peeking through like a solar flare.

"Do you need a snack?"

He doesn't, but pretends he does as he knows to stay in the house now.

"Sure, Mom, I'm gonna go grab my book, though."

"Alright, sweet pea." Mother is back at the sink, oblivious. But, when he is pounding up the narrow wooden stairs to his room, he hears her.

"*Skey umbe!*"

She knows then. But why on earth is she telling it to "Come here right now?"

"My boy, some people call hellish life experience 'bad medicine.' It isn't. I'll tell you what is. Bonewalkers.

"The damage left in the wake of a Bonewalker is beyond anything that even a very cruel person could wish on an enemy. It changes you forever, leaves you filthy with shame. You are left to dance out your life in a series of choreographed symptoms of rage turned inside: addictions, depression, anxiety, apathy.

"Apathy. That is the most dangerous. Apathy has you believe that nothing is worth fighting for or against. That you are not worth fighting for.

"The warriors in this age are the ones who choose to fight. It's not about winning; it's about choosing to stand your ground. That old battle ceremony when you stake yourself to the ground and pledge your life to fight to the death. Your death. Maybe it's more about fighting to the life.

"Bad medicine? Pshaw. *Petchagish!*

"What human possesses the medicine knowledge or the power to inflict that kind of damage? A Bonewalker walks with such arrogance through generations! Leaves a wake of destruction. This is not any kind of medicine. The only medicine exists in the survivors. The new and fearless warriors, Sundancers, Freedom Fighters.

"Crazy eyes, that's how you could tell. He could swallow a 26-ounce bottle of hard stuff. The sign was the eyes of fire. Only if you were astute enough to notice. Eyes full of fear, showing that he was there, but not driving the vehicle; that he knew it.

"In front of that fear, I could see the 'Other,' the Bonewalker, the first I ever saw. It was shooting soulless fury out those eyes.

"I found out the hard way. I did not see the fiery eyes. I made a joke and got smashed in the head for it. Angry at myself for not seeing it, for causing my own pain, I swore to be more vigilant. When you are a kid, you see, you blame yourself.

"You had to be one step ahead. I knew after that to connect the crazy eyes with hellacious suffering."

◉◉◉

The boy is wet and cold. He has had to pee himself and finally poo in his pants, though he has tried so desperately to hold it. The cramps have overtaken him. He silently cries. Why is he in the dark? Where is Mother? He remembers someone putting something over his mouth that tasted terrible and a jab in his arm. Then waking in this dark. He cannot move and feels the ties around his ankles, wrists. Someone is mean. Who is the one who has taken him?

Cold in the cabin, the man builds a fire, then gets the boy's room ready, although in truth there is nothing left to do.

He checks everything for the tenth time knowing the child must be very cold and afraid. Part of him is reticent, knowing the child will be disoriented, frightened.

This is a crucial time. He must form the bond very quickly. He has guarded against possible escape. No one would understand. He walks to the car slowly. He stands for a long time. He will never be ready. He walks to the car. Takes a breath. Opens the trunk.

The Mother wakes, damp from perspiration, gasping for air. She has seen the child. In the trunk of a black car. She has seen a man's hands open the trunk, and as though seeing through that man's eyes, she sees the boy, tied, and curled up on the floor of a stinking trunk. She spends the rest of the night alone at the kitchen table illuminated by the light of street lights. She recalls her Mother's voice and finally understands. "Be mindful for what you pray. You must also pray to be strong enough for the answers that come."

Daylight strikes the boy's eyes, piercing like lightning. It hurts terribly and makes them water as though he is crying. Still blinded he feels hands reach beneath and lift him. The bones in the arms feel hard. It is as if this knocks the wind out of him.

He wills himself not to open his eyes. He hears a door open, feels the warmth inside. Numb, he does not resist any of this. He feels shame for messing his pants; one tear slips out from behind a lid. He hears the steps of the one who carries him. He allows himself to see through squinty eyes, things are upside down from where his head lolls.

Plain wood walls, old furniture, the place is small. The glow and dry heat of a wood stove as they pass. He feels he knows this person from dreams. He is placed gently on a bed, untied.

His mouth is uncovered. He takes big breaths and then lies motionless, eyes closed.

"I am sorry I had to tie you; it was so you didn't hurt yourself."

The boy does not want to show fear, but finally finds the courage to speak.

"Who are you?"

The man is silent for a long while. The child fears he has not been heard, but stills himself, waiting.

"I … am your Father."

◉◉◉

I come from the darkest depth of the space in between. From cold. Nothingness. Black space. There is only a driving need, want. The starving for warmth, blood, heartbeat, flesh.

I must find a host. Walk in your bones. I want the light, need your blood moving heat, to feel the sensation of being alive.

I must be attached to you to feel this. I feed off the hideous possibilities. Dark hunger. This is my lifeblood, my oxygen.

I wait. Wait for a sign of weakness as I stalk my prey. I am patient. Follow until the right moment of detachment, a break in awareness. Then I enter. But you will not know. Your mind will be confused by my sudden presence. Bewilderment so loud that you will be unaware.

I must cling to you long enough that I become you. Your heartbeat, breath, the cells of your body. I become the blood flooding through your veins, an ebbing and flowing red tide driven by the beat of the heart. I become your breath. I become your existence. I become your marrow, I become your bones, as you walk, I walk. I walk in the marrow. I am Bonewalker. I am truly homeless, starving until I find the host. I infiltrate cells, so by the time I am fully integrated, you will be unable to know where you end, and I begin. Like a disease, I eat my way into spirit, become you.

As long as you live, I am alive within you.

I fight to protect the host, to stay within. Cunning, vigilant. My sole purpose is to stay, to keep the host alive.

Heartless, soulless. A vacuum. But within a host, I have a whisper of a heart and soul, an echo of being and, though that is never enough, to satiate it is something.

Control. I battle for control. Until you are no longer yourself, but a shadow of what you once were.

We Bonewalkers are teachers. We teach humans what they would never want to know.

Once, when the Bonewalker wasn't yet fully in possession of him, I caught the real Crazy Eyes outside holding up his hands to the Sky World asking why, why, why over and over. His mask of agony was a terrible thing I hope I never have to witness again. As livid as I always was at him for the pain he had already caused, I felt love at that moment. And some residual part of him knew.

As a young child, the first feeling I can recall having for Dad was fear. I already knew his huge bear paw of a hand could reach down and strike out without cause or warning.

Then there were the confusing nights. I would fall asleep in my blue-flowered baby doll pajamas and wake up naked, searching. I would find them left on the bathroom floor, to my complete confusion. In my teens, I was drugged. I knew because nothing could waken me, and when I did stir, I was in a complete stupor. I once walked barefoot into the winter ocean, so desperate to wash off that inertness. To force me to feel awake.

My nightmares told me the story. I was asleep and something terrible was happening, horrifying enough that I was desperate, fighting to wake up and stop it, but I could never awake. It left me in the cruel grip of a hellish terror that never seemed to abate. Years later, I was told by a doctor that I had bad internal scarring in my back end. I was confused until the quarter dropped.

Sister had left five years earlier at the age of 16, saying Crazy Eyes was looking at her wrong all the time, and she told Mom he was going to rape her. Mom had said, "Yes, you're right, he will. You should leave."

Why would Mom and older sisters let us three younger girls live in that terrible danger? Perhaps they were numb from their own experience. Crazy Eyes was no picnic for them, either. Mother continued to suffer hand-to-hand combat with a man who was trained to kill. We were the enemy. He dished out concussions like a fast-food joint serves burgers on a Friday night.

My Father was a big man, and Bonewalker, I swear, made him even bigger. They can do that. Baseball mitts for hands, and he could swing at you from seemingly across the room and land a good punch. And I still loved him, because I knew it was not him. He was a slave of the Bonewalker.

I heard the raised voices upstairs. My belly tensed, and my heart sped, breath shortening to gasps. I was afraid for Mom. I heard a crash and a silence. Had he finally killed her? I took the basement stairs from my room two at a time, my heart in my throat. I rounded the corner to see Mom cowering in the corner, with Dad leaning over her, hands like claws stretched toward her. Fury fired in me. I spat,

"Don't touch her again, or I'll fucking kill you." There was a terrible tearing inside of me when I said those words. I could see Bonewalker shift, and Father come back to himself. I knew my eyes were on fire. My rage shocked the Bonewalker right out of Father's bones before he had the chance to hurt Mom again.

In that moment, I learned that Bonewalkers are powerless in the face of true courage. How I found the salt I will never know. After most incidents, my Father had no recollection of what he had wreaked and acted as though just yesterday he had not beaten and terrorized one of us into insentience.

I am hoarding all my gifts, my writing, my music, my painting. I put aside these from myself, my enjoyment of life because I am not supposed to savour anything. The gift that could change everything is my self-parole. If I freed myself from this jail, with some conditions, it is the gift that could change everything. But you, my boy? You will be different. I see that already.

◉◉◉

Wild roses are a flower unlike any other. The fragrance of the next world. If innocence had a scent, this would be it. Redolent of sun, honey, earth and sky, purity. Palest pink to deep fiery fuchsia, a delicate golden sunburst of tiny filigree at the centre.

Achingly delicate but tough enough to withstand the winds and rains of May. Wild roses speak of longing for wild places. The breath of the wind, the scent of sunrise, the promise of a new day. Their time is all too soon gone.

I once took Crazy Eyes a single wild rose in the hospital. On his seventh "death bed."

"My battery is running out; I'm a goner."

"No, it's not; you are not."

"How do you know?"

"Because I know things, and this is not your time."

"Even the janitor says I'm pretty much dead."

"Yeah, Dad, 'cause the janitor's qualified to make that call."

At that point, the Bonewalker moved out of his bones again, and that was when I knew it was also powerless in the face of love.

"You have a point, but I know it, this is it."

"Nope, not even close."

"How do you know?"

"You know me, Dad, I just know things."

"You're a good kid. I never deserved you."

"Having kids isn't really about deserving."

"I never understood your ability to love. It scared me."

"That's okay, Dad."

"No, it's not; I knew who you were."

"What do you mean?"

"When you were born, I was told you had been here before, that you were gifted with healing, that you were chosen. A Medicine Carrier. That's why I was so hard on you so that you'd be strong."

"It wasn't only you that was hard on me, the Bonewalker was."

"Who's delusional, you or me? I'm the one with rotten guts, and you are the one talking crazy."

"Yeah, you're right, gangrene can't be fun. And, yeah, I'm talking crazy, but you know I'm right."

"You're right, and I don't know why you still love me."

"Because you brought me into this world; you're my Father."

"I don't deserve to be your Father."

"I am half you, so if I don't love you, there is half of myself I can't love either."

"I guess that's true."

"Yeah, no kidding, look at what I have to look forward to, rotting guts at the age of 70! Here, Dad, I brought you this."

He took the wild rose, deeply inhaled the fragrance, softly moaned in delight. We were transported together, by that wild rose. It held the fragrance of all the wild places he loved. And for a moment it took us there.

"Put it in water."

"Yeah, look, the pill cup is perfect."

Wild roses do not last long once plucked. It is best to enjoy them where they grow, and for the short duration that they bloom riotously signifying the unbroken promise of the coming summer. But I guess when you are trapped in a white man hospital, a lone wild rose will do.

"My boy: it was not only my Father; I have seen others taken over by the dark, by an 'other.' By 'other,' I mean Bonewalker. Bonewalkers are those 'others' that take over people and cause them to do despicable things. I have seen the hosts of Bonewalker grieve their actions after the fact. Bonewalker power is something nobody should witness, especially not children — yet they are the only ones pure enough to fight against it. They fight by being who they are. Harbingers of pure joy."

The man that was no longer a man was hungry. With a dark pervading gnawing that would not relent. It whined and cajoled, begged and bargained. It owned him. Parasitic, it rode inside him unseen, directing his every decision. One could say he was like an animal with this thing attached, but no animal does anything with a single dark purpose.

The being was driven to create darkness where there was light. Pain where there was peace. Rendered vitality to feebleness. Where there was joy it ensured despair. Poisoned affection with hatred. Brought deep shadows at dawn.

If you asked the Bonewalker, it would tell you about loathing and fury. That Bonewalkers are abhorrent. Merciless. Devoid of love. A Bonewalker is every terrible thing you have ever felt inside you, but all at once. A banshee howling within your head could make the ears bleed. It is a ravaging hunger for all things depraved. It is fathomless. A hellish psychic pain so paralyzing it allows taking over hosts easily. While the host is overwhelmed with suffering, Bonewalker moves from inside their bones to do the work of spreading darkness. Like an eclipse that swallows the light. To obliterate, destroy any semblance of clarity. Annihilation is the goal, but slowly, insidiously they creep, they slink forward until the host doesn't know they are no longer in control. They move forward with each doubt; each time the host feels that they are weak, less than, not deserving. Like a kraken, tentacle by tentacle Bonewalkers attach, cell by cell. The victim's only survival is awareness, being fully present. Nobody is. The only thing that drives Bonewalkers away from a new host is constant presence, courage, love.

These dark things have led many, many souls to their death.

Born hungering, the man was an easy host. It had not possessed but became his "spirit" because he had none.

Now was the time to attach, to envelop like a mist, invade like a cancer. And this target being was the boy. The seeds had been planted. Fear was the weapon. And the boy had known fear.

The dark man stands outside in the chill of morning before the sun has touched the spot where he stands by the lake. He smokes, and looks across placid water, but does not see. His mind is not anywhere near as still as the water. He knows the child is sleeping off the effects of the drug, and that he may get sick from it. He tries to recall what food will not upset the stomach of a small boy.

"Oatmeal," he says aloud, and the sound of his voice in the stillness jolts him. He starts the climb as the sun begins to crawl up the mountain with him. He does not stop until he reaches the grave with the pile of stones. He offers tobacco and squats for a time. His prayer is silent. He speaks to the child that lies still. The child does not answer. Neither does Creation.

"I can't stop blaming myself for not coming for you soon enough to revive you. I always will. I have your brother. I will bring the new boy to see you. I wish you were here, but that cannot be helped." He leaves candy that he has brought. Boys like candy.

He walks with sure steps down from the mountain.

The new boy speaks little. He does not look around, ask questions, just looks at the man with quick glances, eyes wide, and staring, unblinking. It unnerves the man.

This boy is like an Old One.

He ensures that the child is warm enough, ensures that he feeds him food that will be easy on his stomach. He has brought books for the child, and toys. The child does not play, and does not read, but sits with the book hour upon hour, turning the pages, too quickly to be reading. The man is very, very patient, and holds the silence with the boy. He feeds the stove to keep the cabin warm. Gives the child plenty of water. Watches him closely for signs of sickness. The child has been silent for a whole day when he speaks.

"Where is my Mother?"

"She is not really your Mother."

"She *is* my Mother."

"No, your Mother died, she was the woman who adopted you."

"Who was my Mother, then?"

"Your Mother was Salteaux, from Manitoba, and Salish. She died when you were a baby."

"How did she die?"

This was the moment. This was the moment to put up the bars of an invisible jail. He waited a long time before answering.

"I killed her."

The child fell silent for many days. He did not stop staring at the man with those big eyes.

◉◉◉

When she was young, she never stopped singing. She sang to herself and knew many of the old songs. She sang in Saulteaux, and he did not understand all the words. He loved to listen to her. She was filled with life, and if she wasn't singing, she was laughing.

She loved bright colours and filled their new home with them. Her husband was happy to walk in the door at night and hear her singing. She had food ready for him because that was the old way. She was a bush girl, and always had a big loaf of baked bannock cooling on the counter when he came in. He always walked over, broke off a chunk, and bit into it. She always laughed and swatted at him. It was their little game. He liked sitting down to eat with her and hearing her talk about work, about the other girls, about what she saw in the store windows. She asked him every night when they were going home. He said, "Not yet, we have to make enough to be able to make it on our own." She knew this, but every night, it was the same thing. She was a good Mother and taught their boy the old songs, and the old ways. He sat silent when she did this. She knew so much more than he did. One night she was not there when he came home, and there was no bannock waiting for him. The house was dark, cold. She had disappeared.

The headlines were cruel, glaring and taunting him at every corner. "*Indian woman found dead on riverbank.*" He did not have to ask the police to know what had happened. That river was a mass, unmarked graveyard for Native women. He knew it was he who had killed her. If he had only listened, taken her home, she would be alive now. Poor, but alive, and the three of them together. He never smiled again, and neither did the boy.

The abducted child's Mother is afraid each time the police come. She knows that they know that she is hiding something. But she feels crazy. Is her feeling real, that the Father took the child? Another child was taken one year before and was never seen or found. She had wondered at that. She had her suspicions about who had stolen her child, but she was afraid to voice them.

At night, she wakes wondering, Could this be who took Krie? Could it be his Father? She is afraid to think of this and stops the flow of thoughts, but like a trapped bird, the one thought wakes her up more than once each night. She keeps those fluttering thoughts in the dark of night to herself. She must not ever speak them.

He's a boy of 10 when his Father moves them from the reserve into Winnipeg. It isn't like Lake St. Martin, or Gypsumville. In the city, he feels like a frightened dog he saw get caught in the fence at the edge of the farm once. The small dog snagged by the barbed wire in its panic had torn its leg down to the bone trying to get loose. The city was noisy, smelly, and confusing. He never knew how to get home. Each day after school he got lost, and Mother had to come looking for him. He thought his Mother was beautiful, but in the city, she looked like a bush Indian. Not like the smartly dressed ones in their high heels with their bright lipsticks and fancy hairdos. She kept her hair long and straight and wore long skirts, and flat shoes. She was still by far the most beautiful of any of the city women. They seemed hard, for all their fancy clothes. Their smiles and laughs had an edge. Like they were tense. Mother was always smiling, with her eyes like dancing fire, and she was always ready with a song, or a tease. It was Mother who made the city bearable. Tired from work in the garage, Father did not come home until late. No laughing with family and friends in the early evenings as he did on the reserve at Lake St. Martin.

As the boy grew to a young man, the city became part of him. He sensed danger in the streets before he confronted it. He learned to know the streets and to walk through them like the old hunters walked the bush back home.

In the cabin, the man unpacks his case. At the bottom are the newspaper clippings. He picks one up. "*Indian Woman found Dead on Riverbank.*" Aloud he says, "Why Indian? How come they never say, 'White Woman found dead here or there?'"

A young Indian woman's body was found in Assiniboine Park, discovered by a fisherman Tuesday morning partly submerged in the water under the footbridge on the Assiniboine River. Upon investigation by the police, it is believed that she was raped, beaten, and drowned. There are no suspects in the case. The victim has not yet been identified.

He flips it over to see the one attached. "*Murder Victim Identified.*"

The woman found two weeks ago Tuesday has been identified as Florence Post (née Gradey) of Lake St. Martin Indian Band, Manitoba. Her husband, John Lawrence Post has been detained

*for questioning. The couple had been living in the city where Mrs.
Post was employed by Johnstone's Linens as a labourer. Mr. Post
works for McLean Auto as a mechanic. No suspects have been
identified.*

The third read *"John Dale Post Not a Suspect."*
   *"Winnipeg Police made a statement today saying that John
Lawrence Post is no longer a suspect in the killing of Florence Post
of Lake St. Martin reserve in Manitoba. Post was found naked in
the Assiniboine River Tuesday, May 12th. Death is presumed to be
by drowning. No further suspects have been identified.*

He picks up another. It is the reserve newsletter on cheap paper,
and the ink is fading.
   *A burial service for the late John Lawrence Post will be held at
the St. Theresa Church graveyard at 11 a.m. Tuesday, March 4,
1971. A feast will follow at the school hall. John Post was prede-
ceased by his wife Florence Post on Friday, February 26, 1968. He
is survived by his only son Dale Post, aged 10, of Winnipeg. In lieu
of flowers, it is requested that donations be made to the Winnipeg
Suicide Hotline."*

One day the man calls the boy from where he is playing outside
the cabin.
   "Let's go for a hike."
   The boy follows wordlessly because he knows he has no
choice. The man finds a path behind the cabin. The boy follows, curious. They climb and climb, and the boy is hot in
the late spring sun, begins to sweat. This burns the wounds
on his bottom, but he keeps climbing because he never has a

choice. He moans quietly, and the man turns, with an expression of concern. The boy's words come out before he can stop them.

"You hurt me, why do you feel sorry for it now?"

Fear floods him, because he knows somehow, that this man will find other ways to hurt him. The man says nothing, but his face looks though it has been crushed, and he climbs more slowly after that. It does not stop the boy's pain, but it lessens a little. They reach the top. The boy looks out across the lake below and sees there is no sign of anyone, any other cabin. His hope departs. They are surrounded by mountains in any direction he looks. Looking at them makes him feel still, and as if he can feel the snowy air of their tops on his skin. The man leads him to a large pile of stones, with a marker.

"This is your brother's grave."

"I have no brother."

"Yes, this is where your little brother is buried."

He is angry now, and yells: "I HAVE NO BROTHER!"

"Yes, say hello to your brother, Ronnie. He was your twin. He died two years ago. If you ever try to leave me, this is what will happen to you." It is then that the boy understands how crazy his captor is and that he must leave.

The boy awakens in the dark to familiar hands. Through the heaviness of sleepiness, he enjoys the waves of pleasure that rise within his body and feels the goosebumps come out on his skin. He sighs. He feels the hands turn him, and his breath stops when the hands become rough. He tenses. The hands reach for his private area. When his bottom is pried apart, he jerks with pain. Agony overwhelms him. It is like a fire. He cries out and begs for the man to stop, but it only makes it worse. The boy is consumed by darkness and goes limp. He is on top of the mountains and feels only the frigid air on his naked skin.

The boy has been quiet all day. Unnerved by the silence, the man finally turns to him when the shadows are long and deep on the cabin walls.

"Do you have a question you want to ask me?" How did he know?

"Yes. What ... is your name?" The boy stares at him, unwavering. The man feels as though he has been hit by a rock. Before he can think about it, his lips open and the name spills out and drops to the floor.

"Dale Post."

◉◉◉

The boy has been exploring around the bush. The man does not bother with him, so he begins to seek and find the way. He finds a game trail that follows the road.

He walks as far as he can until the man calls him back. He has found treasure.

The boy knows he will need food and water, something to carry it all in. The next time the man goes for a shopping and laundry trip, he will begin. He does not show that he is impatient waiting for the man to leave.

"Father, will you bring me some chocolate from town next time?"

The man does not smile, but the boy senses he is pleased. This is why he has called him "Father." As a weapon. He only wants to know when the man will leave, as he has seen him make the preparations.

"Yes, I will bring it back tomorrow."

For the first time since he has been taken, the boy feels powerful. He is filled with knowing that he will hurt this man, now. The man will be very angry when he finds him gone. He imagines the look of realization and then sheer horror. He laughs inside his belly, silently, as he sees how the man will quickly run through the cabin, calling his name, and run outside. He laughs harder within when the man begins running through the bush and finally up the mountain to the grave. That is when he sees himself running as hard as he can down a path he has found that follows the road. He will be running for his life, and he will be laughing silently in his belly all the way.

The time comes, finally. The car has gone; the boy has waited until he can no longer hear the crunching of the tires on the gravel in the deep silence. He waits until the man has had enough time to turn around for something forgotten, though he never has, then packs slowly and deliberately and has no need of rushing; knows exactly how much time he has. Dead calm and sure of his plan; he tells himself that he is ready; but part of him does not want to leave. He pushes those thoughts down and takes a deep breath. He puts his backpack on, selects the warmest blanket, grabs the last apple from the bowl and closes the front door behind him. He stands and looks at the lake, farther to the mountains. He walks to the shoreline; he likes the sound of the small stones crunching beneath his running shoes.

The ice has all gone along the shoreline where it used to crust around the reeds. Little fish dart and flash. He puts the apple on the blanket. He picks up a stone and skips it as hard as he can. It plops. He finds another. It skips six times, and he puts his arms in the air, cheering so loudly that the echo comes back. He adjusts his backpack and takes a big bite of the apple. Sweet juice runs down his throat. He walks down the road and into the bush where he finds the tree, which he climbs to the place he has decided he will wait. His backpack hangs in the heavy foliage, while he lolls across the large branch and stretches like a lion. He hangs upside down like a monkey, by his knees. He sits, squashed up, like a bird, wishing he had clawed feet to grasp the bark. This is the safest place. Mom has said that she was taught that no one ever looks up. He lays down in the open arms of the tree and falls asleep.

The sound of tires and lights jabbing the dark awaken him. He listens to the engine turning off, the car door opens, the trunk opens. He hears the squeak of the front door open, followed by the back and forthing of an oblivious someone unloading a car. Then he hears the trunk slam. He does not hear the front door close, but he hears the man's yell.

"Krie!" The voice is choking. He giggles. He does not hear the man but feels that he is running around looking for him as he hears him yell his name repeatedly. He has not heard fear like this in a voice. He snickers and then quiets. Feet crunch on the beam of light over the gravel; now he must be quiet. The light goes up and down, in all directions like a mad thing. He hears the man sob. He feels sad for him.

The man is crying like a child. He listens to the voice and when he hears it going up the trail, up and up, he makes his move. Carefully climbing down, he hits the trail jogging, knowing that a full-out run will wear him out. He jogs for hours until he knows he is safe to rest. He makes a nest like a bird in a big tree, and he sleeps.

It feels cold, but the birds singing all around him in the pre-dawn light is the most beautiful sound he has ever heard. He drinks water and eats some nuts and raisins. He pees, watching the steam rise off the leaves below. It's time, but there is no need to run. He knows he cannot be seen from the road. He walks all day, and still, he is beside the road.

When he hears the car slowly crawling down the road, he freezes, then goes deeper into the bush, finds a good tree and climbs. He stays still until he hears the car go back the other way. He continues on his way, only finding the main road at sundown. Now he must make a choice. A road has to lead somewhere. He closes his eyes, takes a breath. Asks, "Which way?" This has worked in the past. He has found lost treasures, even small ones, and knows that the voice within will tell him.

He waits, patiently. "Right." He goes on sure feet and walks in the deep culvert on the side of the road. He will not be seen.

The man has been in a blind panic since discovering the boy is missing. He must find him, and he must get him back. He sobs uncontrollably and rages. The cabin is a ruin of smashed furniture. He must find the boy or it will be too late. Panic owns him, and this he must kill.

The boy sniffs the air. Smoke. Grilling meat. His stomach grumbles. He hears voices through the bush, sees the sideroad. He walks, weak with hunger, and wants real food. The white men, dressed in camouflage, sit around a fire with cans in their hands. They talk loud and do not notice him at first. The biggest man stands and says, "Kid, where the hell did you come from?" The lie falls easily from his lips. He looks straight into the man's eyes and the man turns, finds his phone, and dials. The police arrive within the hour. Now he is safe.

He tells the police everything. Well, almost everything. He leaves out the part where he saw his captor in a photograph dressed in the same uniform as them. He thinks that this may not be a good thing to share. The officers are white-faced and tight. He tells them everything he can think of when they ask him question after question. When he speaks of the night, one of them has tears in his eyes and looks down. The other turns away quickly. The third pounds the table and the boy jumps.

The policeman apologizes.

"It's okay," the child says, though it isn't.

They buy him a hamburger and French fries, a chocolate milkshake, and a Crispy Crunch bar. This food is the best food he has ever eaten.

The ring sounds important. She tears off her rubber gloves and hits her head on the open cupboard door as she runs to get the phone. Mother chokes through words that don't register at first. She does not want to have hope, but her heart sings – dances – when they tell her that this may be her Krie.

She cannot respond until they ensure she has heard. She is on the plane to Whitehorse before she allows herself to believe it is him. She has looked at the faxed photograph maybe hundreds of times.

Within her core, ice melts slowly, and the tears flow down her face for the entire flight.

She can barely breathe as the policewoman turns off the engine of the RCMP cruiser.

Her chest tightens more as they walk into the detachment.

When Krie sees her, he looks with a straight and unwavering look. She sees him almost fly into her arms. He clings to her like a little monkey and does not want to leave her. When she signs the documents, he stands very close. They will leave this afternoon, as the man has not been caught. She has booked a trip to Disneyland. It will not be safe to go home, they have advised.

Mother does not ask him questions. His heart expands, and he loves her more for the feeling, like tears flooding his heart. He does not want to answer the questions anymore. He does not want to remember.

That night he wakes screaming, and she rolls over to gently hold him close. He will not let go of her all night. He sleeps all the first day. She lets him and does not wake him to eat. She knows he will eat when he needs to. They don't leave the Disney-themed motel room for two days, and she reads by the window but looks up to see the little form in the bed, breath barely rising and falling. Never again, she thinks, never again will you ever be harmed. Over my dead body.

Krie is finally ready to go out to the theme park, to the rides, and timidly holds her hand as they walk around. He cannot decide which ride to go on. He decides on the Haunted Mansion. When a figure suddenly jumps out in the dark, he screams. He does not stop. When they emerge to the light, she sees he has peed his pants. She wordlessly ties his hoodie around his tiny waist. Without speaking they return to the room. He plays quietly on the floor for the rest of the day. She looks at old photos of him on her cell phone; he is always smiling and laughing. She wills that child back. Using spells she does not know; she calls him to her.

The June heat came and with it nightly thunder and lightning storms that rolled back and forth across the sky. Krie thought it sounded like someone bowling up there and lightning was a full strike. Someone up there was good bowler judging by the number of forks that he saw flashing through the windows.

The storms both energized and frightened him. In the middle of the night, he was fearful that the old house would be hit and burst into flames. He lay in the heavy heat, with just a cotton sheet over him, and tried to listen for the night trains. The trains wailed low, and he loved the sound. It made him miss things he didn't even know. It spoke the words of his deep heart.

At the end of June, Mother and he were enjoying homemade lemonade in the yard. He liked the canopy of vines that Mother had planted. He liked peering up at the sun shards glinting between thickly tangled vines that looked like the sprawling fingers of a wizard. Mother spoke after a very long silence.

"Krie, how would you like to meet your Grandmother?"

"I have a Grandmother?"

"Yes, you have a lot of family."

"I would like to meet my Grandmother. What is her name?"

"Her name is Sopiah Red Sky."

"I like that name – I love thunder, but it scares me a little."

Grandmother was due the following week. She was to stay in the spare room. Krie carefully chose flowers from the garden and put them beside her bed. His heart was pounding when he saw the taxi stop out front. He searched for the face of the woman who was his Mother's Mother. He saw a black head with grey streaks emerge from the back of the taxi. He saw long hair and a tall woman. He said, "She must really like bannock, Mother." Mother giggled. He watched as she stood on the sidewalk looking at the house. He waved and ran outside. He stopped in front of her, looked up into eyes, and it was like looking in his own.

He could not speak. He felt her eyes hold him very close. She felt familiar, and he felt very, very safe. Her eyes held him so close that it was as if he were in her arms asleep. She was smiling and her eyes were gentle and twinkly. Her brown face, framed by long, straight black hair was beautiful, he thought. Her smooth skin was used to smiling. He could see the smile lines everywhere.

Her cheekbones were high, and she had even teeth, white against her creamy brown skin. She knelt and opened her arms. A magnet lured him forward. He was enveloped in warmth.

She held him gently, but he felt she wanted to hold him very tight. He put his head against her and held her back, his little arms only reached her sides. He hugged her hard, and never wanted to let her go. She made cooing noises very quietly, rocking him gently to and fro, to and fro, to and fro. It was like being in a human hammock. It made him sleepy-safe. The tears on his cheeks were not from sadness; they were a story for her; a story of his heart.

When he stood away, she reached to his hand that was brushing the tears away and said, "Allow your tears to fall." The second before she said this, he already knew it. And he knew this was the way it was going to be with the two of them.

Grandmother had many gifts for him and many photographs. She introduced him to his family. She told him a story. This story made Mother cry. She is not his Mother; she is his Auntie. His Mother is in hospital. He looked at photographs of Aunts, cousins, and finally his blood Mother. He held the photograph and took a deep breath.

He looked nothing like her. She was very beautiful. She had long, flowing hair, was throwing her head back, laughing. She was slim, but like Grandmother was tall, and had high, lovely cheekbones. She had big brown eyes and a long nose that turned up at the end. Her full lips and even teeth made her the young version of Grandmother.

"What is her name? She is beautiful!"

"Leah, and yes, she is my boy, inside and out."

"Why didn't she want to come?"

"She is not well, my boy."

"Does she have the flu?"

"No, my boy, she has a troubled mind."

"Will I meet her soon?"

"It may not be for some time, but I know she wants to and that she loves you very much!"

"Can I send flowers home for her?"

"We can put something out for her. She will get it in another way."

"How?"

"I will show you, my boy, we have lots of time."

He felt that everything she said was true. Grandmother was never going to lie to him. In bed that night, he heard voices from the kitchen. Later, he heard Grandmother scolding her daughter.

"Mariah. You should not have let him think you were his mother!"

"I wanted once, Mom, for a child to call *me* Mom."

"It isn't *fair* to him; he needed to know the truth."

"The truth is too ugly for a child."

""The truth is what it is, we all have to bear our own."

"I just couldn't, Mom. I couldn't do it." Grandmother's voice became kind.

"Alright, Mariah, alright, I understand, but we have to make this right now, he has a Mother, and you're his Auntie. Nobody is going to take that away from you, or the bond you have."

"Mom, he is the only child I'll ever have." Now he heard Mom/Auntie crying hard. His chest hurt for her.

"I know, sweetheart, I know, but we must all do what is right for the child and that is to tell him the truth."

"How can a child bear a truth that terrible?"

"My girl. Life is such that we all bear terrible truths."

Krie began to wake up much earlier when he found that Grandmother was always up before him. Compelled to look out to the back garden one morning, just before dawn, he saw her outside. She stood facing where he knew without knowing that the sun would come up. She had a drum, which she was beating gently. She began to sing. Krie stayed hidden, to watch. He did not want to disturb her. Somehow, he understood the words of the language he had never heard. She was greeting the sun. When she was done, she took a pinch of something in her left hand from a pouch at her waist and held it up. She spoke very quietly and put what was in her hand on the ground. It all seemed so special, and it felt as though she was having a private conversation that was only hers. He watched for four days. On the fifth, he heard her say, "I know you're there, Krie, come out." He did, and from then on, each morning this was their special time. He learned that this was the way she kept connected to an old ceremony that happened each summer.

Grandmother and Mother/Auntie were in the kitchen having tea when Krie came down from his schoolwork. He had enjoyed their voices fluttering like birds up the stairs to where he had been studying.

"Are you finished already, Krie?"

"Yes, Mother ... Auntie." She winced.

"Would you like a snack?"

"Sure, Auntie."

"Grandmother, what is that you are eating on your bannock?"

She giggled like a little girl.

"It's peanut butter mixed with honey, not very traditional, I'm afraid." Grandmother was laughing, too.

He enjoyed some and asked for seconds.

"So, Mariah, what do you think?" asked Grandmother.

"I think it is a great thing, and I think it's Krie's decision."

"Krie," Grandmother said, her voice going up at the end like a question, "Would you like to come to ceremonies with me?"

"I'd go anywhere with you, Grandmother." She smiled her beautiful smile, and it made his insides dance.

"Good, then we will sew your ribbon shirts."

Grandmother and Auntie were in the kitchen surrounded by a lake of bright fabrics and ribbon when he came down from school the next noontime. Grandmother called to him.

"Come here, my boy," she said, holding a partly made shirt to his chest.

"Perfect," both women said, and then they laughed.

"Tea, Mom?"

"Yes, please, and we should put some out. Krie, take the cup of tea and put it under the big tree out back, will you, my boy?" This he did without question.

By the end of the day, there was a beautiful shirt for him, royal blue with streaming yellow, red, and white ribbons. Over the next few days, there were several of them, all different, and all beautiful. They hung in his closet, and when he looked at them, he had a warm glow in his belly.

It was called a Powwow and Gramma, Auntie and Krie were standing while the grass dancers blessed the arbour.

"Grass Dance is very old, Krie. Long ago, they would have been tamping down long grass out on the land for the people to gather like this. This dance is a lot like a prayer. They are supposed to match moves with each side of their body, one after the other; you see that?"

The regalia had fringes that ran from wrist to armpit and all down the sides of the legs. Everyone had different colours. After the song was done, they stayed standing for something called the Grand Entry. A line of men with flags and staffs danced in. Behind them, he had heard the announcer say, were the Golden Age Men, and Women. The men looked fierce, and the women danced like grass in the wind. They looked very serious.

"Gramma, why do they not smile?"

"It is to show dignity."

"What is dignity?"

"It is something that means a great deal to our peoples. The men are showing how they are ready to protect their people, and the women are walking gently on Mother Earth, and showing how they protect the people in this way. These things mean everything to them, so it is something to be serious about. As they dance, it is a prayer. With each sway of the Grandmothers' fringes, it is a prayer. With each movement of the Grandfathers, it is a prayer."

As the Adult, Teen, Junior and Tiny Tots categories were introduced, Krie was often overcome. There was so much colour, noise, and movement that he had to close his eyes several times. The colour was as loud as the drums over the loudspeakers. He listened as the MC introduced each dance category. Grandmother bent to explain each dance style to him. Each was beautiful, but when the junior boys traditional came in front of them, he said, "Grandmother, that is how I will dance."

She smiled her beautiful smile. "Well then, my boy, I know what I will be doing all this winter."

"What?"

"Beading, my boy, beading the most beautiful junior boy's regalia that will ever be seen."

He felt her love like a warm quilt. He felt a new sense within like butterflies were dancing to a breeze skipping along the top of a lake. It changed when he saw him. His chest tightened so that he could not breathe, and joy was overshadowed by shock and fear in the silence.

Dale Post was dancing past, right in front of where they sat, dressed in men's traditional regalia! Krie could not speak. He sat frozen and felt the goosebumps come out on his skin. He did not speak of it until Auntie asked him if he was feeling alright.

"He is here, Auntie. The man who took me is here. I remembered his name. Dale Post is dancing."

The police car was at their motel by the time they arrived. Krie carefully described Dale Post's dance outfit the best he could remember. Grandmother and Auntie said nothing but did not leave his side. He did not see the man again but was watching for him for the next two days.

"It's Inter-tribal time!" boomed the announcer's voice across the grounds to where they sat, under a shade. Grandmother rose and invited Krie with her eyes. He did not hesitate. The drums called and pulled, and he walked with her and Mother out onto the arbour. The drums spoke to him, told him to answer their call with his feet; echo them with the movement of his body. He was lost in the dancing. The sun was gentle on his face. A breeze caressed him. He saw nothing except the colour moving all around him. He felt part of it, part of everything. The earth beneath his feet was alive. There was only him, his heart matching the beat of the drum, his body swaying, the sun, the breeze, and the greatest peace and joy his heart had ever known.

The police returned the next night, late, at the motel. Krie was asleep. When he woke in the morning Krie did not know if it was a dream, or if he heard correctly.

"Ma'am, we looked up this name the boy gave. Dale Post served in the RCMP. He was born in Manitoba. Trouble followed him. There were a lot of allegations. Misconduct, assault, both women and children. Nothing could be substantiated. He was watched by Internal Affairs for a long time. Then he disappeared, around 1985. The Whitehorse detachment closed the file after about five years. They found and matched remains to him two years later. A cold case. Dale Post is dead, ma'am."

"Mother, what does this mean? Did Dale have a brother?"

"No, it is him."

"How could it be, they found his remains!" Auntie's voice was disbelieving and had a sharp edge of fear.

"Mariah, there are strange things in this world and between this world and the next. I was afraid of this, something I felt in my gut. Dale Post is what my people call 'Dead who walk among us,' and we must never speak his name again."

"I'm not sure that I understand."

Sopiah took a pencil from her purse and wrote on a paper. She slid it across to Mariah. On it was one word, "Bonewalker." Mariah could only stare at it, frozen.

They had settled on a blanket inside a large hall.

Krie had on his best shirt and a pair of brand-new moccasins that Grandmother and Auntie had made. He liked the little bear-track designs beaded on their tops and the smoky smell of the hide. He watched and listened very carefully.

Two men with long braids down their backs were setting up things on a large fur robe in the middle of the room. Grandmother said it was a buffalo robe altar with sacred items. The man with two braids took a large shell with something burning in it. He went to people one by one, and they washed themselves in the smoke. When it came to Krie, he did the same as the others and wished with all his might that he could be ready for what was going to happen.

He felt alive in the moment and as if there was nothing on his mind but now – this place, and this time. When the Medicine Man entered, Krie felt him before he came into view. There was something different about this man. As if he knew too much. He had a clean sort of feel about him. The man sat on a chair and another man called out: "If you have a request of Walking Wolf, please make a line, and you will have private time to make your requests."

Grandmother took Krie to the line-up. When it was their turn, the man rose and embraced her. "Sopiah, it's so good to see you."

"Krie Red Sky, this is Walking Wolf, Elmer Johns." The man looked both old and young to Krie, something about the cleanness made him look young. His eyes, where Krie could see the knowledge, looked old. He patted Krie on the head. Grandmother gave a pouch of something to the man. He took it, and it was placed in a basket with many pouches. She spoke to Walking Wolf at length and told the story of how Krie was taken, his trials, his escape, and the things the police had said. He nodded; head turned while looking at the floor.

"You have a powerful spirit, Krie. It is time for you to have a name. We'll make things right for you. When you know your name, you will have a direction to travel in your life and will know how to reach the power that you have within."

The man's voice was hypnotizing. Krie roused himself to give his thanks.

"*Meegwetch*, Grandfather, *meegwetch.*" A look passed between Elmer and Grandmother as they smiled at one another and nodded an understanding.

The ceremony transported Krie to a place he had never been. Within the absolute darkness of the room, he was stirred by songs in a language he had never heard. He floated on those songs and the prayers in between.

At one point, the ceremony man's voice reached through the darkness. He spoke about a person's life, their suffering, and that his name was "Bear Child." He said the name in a language Krie did not know. He spoke of the power of this name, the colours that went with this name, and offered that the owner of this name would need to understand his gifts.

"These gifts are not easy to carry. You will sometimes bless these gifts, at other times curse them. You will know things that others can only guess at. You will feel things that others do not. You will know things to come that you do not want to know, and other times, it will be a good thing to know these things. Learn to work with these gifts. Never be afraid of them."

Krie knew that it was he whose name was now Bear Child. He spoke into the dark, reached his voice back, "Thank you, Grandfather, I will do as you have said. *Meegwech.*"

When the lights came back on, Krie woke up. He did not know if he had been dreaming, but it did not matter. He knew his name and that was all that he needed to know.

The next morning, when he greeted the sun with Grandmother and they said their prayers, he used his name, just as Grandmother always had. She smiled widely, and he felt brand new. Now, nothing would be the same again.

The man that was no longer a man was hungry. It was a dark pervading gnawing that would not let him alone. It whined and cajoled, begged and bargained. It owned him. Parasitic, it rode on his back unseen and directed his every decision.

Krie screamed everyone awake, including himself. Both Grandmother and Auntie came running, sleep-tousled.

"What's wrong, my boy?" they asked together.

"It came in my dream; it was trying to pull the life out of me."

"What was it?" Grandmother's face was frowning, serious.

"It was the man, but more than the man."

"Dale Post?"

"The man who is not a man, who took me, but it is not a man."

"What is it?"

"It is a black blob on his back. It is black and shiny and looks like a tadpole. It makes him do the things."

"What things, my boy?"

"All the bad things. The thing makes Dale Post do the bad things."

"Did it say anything?"

"Yes. It misses bone games. It wants to walk in my bones."

Krie overheard, although he tried not to.

"Mariah, I think we need to take him to the bone game tournament. He needs to learn how to play. There is something of the sacred in it."

"Yes, I think you are right, and it may be a good distraction for all of us."

"Well, it never hurts one to be around drumming and singing."

Krie could hear the drums as soon as he got out of the car. The rapid beat made him feel good and happy. He felt the excitement building in him. Although curious, he was still a little afraid around other people, so he reached out for Auntie and Gramma's hands. He was wearing his light blue ribbon-shirt and worried a little that others would not be dressed in this way. They were. Not only that, but it appeared they were dressed in their best. They entered the gym, and the drums were loud, and there were people dressed in hide vests with beadwork, ribbon shirts, ribbon dresses. It was colourful and beautiful. Everyone was smiling. The aroma of bannock and coffee hung in the air.

"Now Krie, get ready for the other team. They will yell, point, dance wildly or make other body gestures; they will hammer on drums and sing their war songs. They will laugh, and jeer, and make strange expressions, look at you in what my Grand-mother called 'a bad tone of face.' They will do war cries, look fierce, all to take your mind off the game, and what your instinct is telling you."

There was no time here. Just the sense of fun, community. Krie forgot all about his ordeal that usually whispered doubt in his ear. Grandmother and Mariah watched him with tears in their eyes. Radiant, laughing, as he faked out team after team until his team won each bout. They stood together with their prizes, and Krie looked like the little boy that he had been before the shadows of what had happened; before the darkness had touched his life. When he fell asleep in the car on the way home, Grandmother whispered to Mariah, "This is beyond the resilience of a child. This one is so gifted. This one is so spe-cial."

"I know, Mom. I know."

◉◎◉

When Krie woke up he felt something wrong. A heaviness in the house. He heard Grandmother getting up for the dawn prayers, and made himself ready. Shivered as he pulled on a warm sweater, he sensed a deeper silence than before. Grandmother smiled when she saw him in the kitchen. They smiled back at one another.

In the garden during prayers, there was a loud buzzing, vibration in the air above him. Krie opened his eyes to see a hummingbird right in front of him. It flew over his head, back and forth, wind dancing. The gentle fan of its feathers moved at lightning speed. His heart danced with the tiny bird's movement. There was joy, excitement, and a thrill of magic that went through him like sweet freshwater. The tiny creature was there the entire time of the prayers. It was a good thing because what they found in the house later needed magic to come before its discovery.

The coroner was a woman and was strangely cool in the face of the sight of Mariah lying cold and still in a tangle of blankets.

"It would appear she died in her sleep."

"She struggled, so it may have been a heart attack. Did she suffer from asthma?"

"No." Grandmother was stoic.

"Well, it seems she had an attack of something, judging by the way she is all tangled in the bedding."

Grandmother had a look of determination. There was sadness but, in her eyes, Krie could see the fire of anger that he had only seen once before. It was when he told her about seeing Dale Post.

She was resolute when she made the calls. Walking Wolf came the next day.

"Bear Child, how are you?" he asked but he looked as though he already knew.

"I'm okay, thank you, Grandfather, but I am sad that my Auntie has gone."

"Be strong, and cry when you need to. Grief is a journey we take together as a family and yet alone. Each person feels it in a different way. Do you know what will help you?"

"I think the morning prayers, Grandfather. They always make me feel part of everything; Grandmother taught me to connect to all that is after I am done."

"That's good my boy, that's good, and I am here to help and to listen."

"Thank you, Grandfather, it is good to see you. Let me make you some tea."

Grandmother and Uncle smiled at one another. Krie busied himself, but nothing he could do could take the heaviness off his chest.

"Grandmother, what will happen if something happens to you?"

"Well, nobody in our family is living a healthy enough life to care for you, but there is someone."

"Who, Grandmother?"

"You will meet him tomorrow; he is coming in from Whitehorse. He's a bush Indian – knows everything about that land."

"Is he family?"

"He may as well be."

It was still dark when Krie was woken by a voice in the kitchen he did not recognize. That was happening a lot these days. The stranger spoke like he was from someplace else, with expressions that Krie had never heard. He was fascinated. He knew who it was before he entered the kitchen. The man stood, coffee cup in hand, leaning on the counter, one foot tucked behind the other. So, this was Haywire. He rubbed his brown face and tidied the front of his greying hair by running one hand through it. His hands were scarred and muscled, forearms lean and strong looking. Not a tall man, he had a presence. He stood as if he was trying not to be noticed, but his presence was so strong, he would stand out anywhere. He wore jeans and a cowboy shirt rolled up to below his elbows. As lean as a man can be without looking thin, his body seemed as hard as a rock. Light on his feet, he walked to the stove to get more coffee without making a sound. In those broad shoulders, Krie sees the muscle and sinew moving. He wanted to look like that when he was a man.

Haywire glanced at Krie on the way back from the stove. Krie could tell the man had sensed his presence. He looked Krie straight in the eyes, without fear or reserve. It was like being eye-to-eye with a wild animal, measured intelligence and pure wild. He kept his hair short; it was dark brown laced with grey. His eyes were cinnamon, and they were kind. He had a shy smile; there was warmth in his eyes. He broke contact when he smiled and look down like he had a secret with himself. That smile made Krie see what Haywire must have looked like as a boy.

"Call me Haywire. I knew you long before you were born."

"Haywire?"

"It's my nickname, what people like to call me."

"Why?"

"It's an expression from the Yukon, ah, let's say it's for someone who takes risks and likes adventures."

"And – how could you know me before I was born?"

Haywire hesitates.

"I know your Mom. Really well."

"What is she like?"

Haywire sits with this question and doesn't speak for a minute or two, sadness crossing his eyes like a moose in a meadow.

"She's the most beautiful woman I have ever known," he says, looking older and more tired than before.

"So, what about your name? You tell people your Nation before they get to ask you."

"I know, but it was the name Leah gave me. And let's give you a nickname!"

"Well, let's give you another name."

"What name?"

"It could be prosecuting attorney."

"Why? What is that?"

"Let's hope you never have to know that." He is grinning, Grandmother laughing, and Krie wishes he were older, so he could be part of this.

"Well, I have to get to know you and find what I like about you the most – kind of the thing that makes me laugh."

"Oh? Did Mother have a nickname?"

"Oh yes ... Chaos."

"Why?"

"Well, she forgot a lot of things; like her mind travelled too fast. She was always losing things."

"Like her mind?" Silence.

"Well, she just put that in her Indian suitcase for a while, is all."

"What else was she like before the Bonewalker?" He did not see Haywire move, but he felt the shift.

"This one didn't fall far from the tree!" the women nodded.

"She brought happiness. Like a bear cub rolls and plays, she made people laugh. People up my way loved her; she made everyone come together, forget they had grudges.

"What's a grudge?"

"Something people should never have in their cache."

"What's a cache?"

"Where we keep our food, so the bears can't get at it."

"Where do you live?"

"Well, Camp Robber, I live on a river in a place called Tagish."

"Camp Robber? I know I'm not allowed to steal."

"No, camp robber is a little bird who sits right next to you in the bush and is the most curious thing around."

"Oh. Is that my new nickname?"

"You earned it fair and square. How would you like to come with me and learn to be an Indian?"

"Yeah!" Krie's eyes sparkled – a lake in the sun.

"Well, you can come with me back to the Yukon after all this is done, what do you say?"

"Grandmother?"

"Yes, Krie, I think it would be a good thing, I can't teach you how to be a man after all, and men's teachings have to come through men."

Krie was worried about Grandmother. She wasn't looking well. Haywire said it was the sadness of losing her child. Krie watched her carefully, and the shadow man was watching Krie.

After carefully folding all his clothes, Krie looked around at his room. He would miss this place, and he would miss his Auntie-Mom. She stood in the door as he packed and looked serious. He looked at her, and then she was gone.

Walking Wolf was in the kitchen with Grandmother and Haywire. They were talking quietly and stopped when Krie walked in. He backed out, and Walking Wolf called him back.

"So, Bear Child, I hear you are moving up North!"

"Yes, Grandfather, I am going to learn to be a man."

"Well, that's a good thing. Can I come with you?"

"Sure, Grandfather."

"No, Grandson, I don't think I am ready to be a man at my age. But are you ready, my boy, to be very brave?"

"I'm not sure, Grandfather."

"Well, the Bonewalker has chosen you, so you will have to be."

Krie looked at Grandmother and Haywire. Grandmother's face was serious, and Haywire was looking at him hard.

"My boy, Bonewalkers only take on a worthy opponent."

"I don't know what you mean."

"A Bonewalker likes to play with people, but they do not waste their time with a weak person who can't put up a good fight."

"I can try, Grandfather."

"I know you will, my boy. You have to believe in your own power."

"Like when that guy in the cartoon points to his ring and says 'Shazam,' and lightning comes out of it?"

"Yes, it's like that, only that the power comes from inside you."

"How will I know how to find the power?"

"The power will be there when you need it. It knows when to come to you."

"Will it do the fighting for me?"

"Your power will help you, but it will take a lot of focus. You know how you focus on hard schoolwork?"

"Yes, I have to think of only the work, not the birds singing, or someone mowing their lawn, or little kids playing outside."

"That's it, my boy, your job is to believe in that power and think only of what you are trying to do."

"I will try hard, Grandfather."

"You won't be alone. Wolverine Claw will be with you, and we will all be praying. A lot of praying and ceremonies will be done for you.

"Who's Wolverine Claw?"

"That's me, Camp Robber; it's my clan name. You will learn a lot about those things up North."

"Okay, Haywire, when should I be ready."

"Well, if you are going to be a bush Indian, you need to be born ready."

"Was I Grandmother?"

All three said it at once: "Yes, my boy."

The others did not mention seeing Mariah. The day he and Haywire were leaving, Grandmother looked at Krie for a long time.

"Is someone there that you are looking at? I've noticed since Mariah passed that you seem to focus on someone who is not there."

"She is here, Grandmother, she is here all the time." Grandmother smiled her beautiful smile, and her eyes filled.

"Thank you, my boy, for telling me. I can sense her, but not see her. I am glad. It means she is fine and will find her way home."

"Yes, Grandmother, she is only waiting for me and Haywire to leave."

The time had come. Krie did not want to leave Grandmother, but he knew that she felt the same, and it somehow made it easier. The taxi was waiting, and they were all out by the road. He and Grandmother held each other close for a long time. Neither wanted to let go. Finally, Haywire spoke.

"Sorry, but if we don't go now, that sun will leave without us; we want to make it out of the mountains by sundown."

Krie waved as long as he could see Grandmother. She got smaller and smaller, but he could see her arm waving in a large arc. He waved back looking through the small pickup window. Then they were on their way.

◉◎◉

Haywire didn't speak much when they were driving to Hope. Krie knew it was because of the traffic. He didn't imagine there was much traffic in the Yukon by the sounds of things. When they hit the foothills just by Bridal Falls, Haywire seemed to relax. As they made their way up the Coquihalla, Krie felt free. As though all the heaviness of the grief and the bad things that had happened were not anywhere close by. He hoped that it would stay that way.

Krie noticed the crows in Abbotsford and didn't think much about it until he kept seeing them up in the mountains and beyond.

He finally asked Haywire, "Have you been watching the crows?"

"Yeah, I sure have, I think they are excited that you are coming; they will probably tell the Ravens, and then the Raven clans will know that you are on your way."

"Why?"

"Ravens and Wolves work together. Hunt together. Your Mom was adopted by the Wolf clan, so you will be Wolf. There are many clans, but these are two main ones that tell people who they can marry or not, and how everyone is related."

"Oh; well, I think I am going to like being a Wolf." Haywire smiled for the rest of the way North.

"Have you walked up on top of it?"

"Many times, so has your Mother. It's part of my family trapline."

"You trap up there?"

"No, we hunt up there."

"Oh, well, will we go up there, too?"

"Sure, we are going to go all over this land. You'll be following in your Mother's footsteps. She loved the whole thing."

"Then I will, too."

They drove up what looked like a bush road about sundown. Turned a corner, and there was a house with smoke coming out of a stovepipe.

"We'll stop here for an early dinner and the night; my cousin will have it ready." Haywire rapped twice on the door before calling out. He turned back to Krie.

"May as well get you splitting wood. I'm going to find, Lorna."

Krie liked the feeling of the hatchet splitting the wood in two, and worked carefully, remembering his instructions. A chill gripped him, and a numbness came soon after, from his toes to his head. He was afraid he would throw up, and he stopped. He stood, his body swaying in a circle, hoping this would pass.

What came next was like a video in front of his eyes, and his chest tightened with the feeling of something terrible. Haywire turned and saw Krie bent and gripping his knees, sweating, and panting; hard; eyes shut tight.

"Krie, what is it?"

"I saw my Mom, and a man with black hair, and an axe. It was like it was in slow motion. I saw her raise the axe, the man fighting for it. Then it fell. Both Leah and the man fell, and there was a lot of blood!"

"Take deep slow breaths, Krie, it will pass."

"But the blood."

"Breathe in, good, hold it a little, okay, out. In, hold it a little, there you go."

Krie came back to himself and felt tired again like he needed to sleep.

"It was the Bonewalker. He hurt Mom and I couldn't do anything."

"It was long ago, Krie. Even I couldn't do anything."

"Did Mom kill my Father?"

"Krie, the Bonewalker killed him."

"I miss my Mom." Hot tears spilled over.

"I know, Krie, but it won't be forever. It won't be long before she will be better, you have to trust."

"It's hard."

"Oh, boy, I know it."

"You miss her, too."

"More than anyone will ever know."

At daybreak, Krie was full of excitement. Haywire was taking him hunting for the first time. He checked his little backpack again, made sure he had extra socks, water.

"Salt and matches; always pack salt and matches, wherever you go. I don't care if you are in the city. Always."

"Why is that?"

"Salt for if you sweat a lot walking up and down mountains. And for any fresh game. Matches, because you never know where you have to spend the night, and fire heats and protects out in the bush."

"Okay, I will make sure I take everything you tell me to."

Krie did not see Haywire's gentle smile.

"After this, I will stop answering your questions. I will let you figure the answer out yourself. If I tell you to do something, you will have to trust me it's for a good reason, okay?"

"There is a lot to learn, right, Haywire?"

"I'm still learning; and it doesn't help that the whole world is changing."

Krie made sure his bootlaces were tight. They were still sticky from the dubbin that Haywire had showed him how to put on. He made sure that he packed up coffee, tea, and sugar, as he had been told.

He was curious about everything but did not ask any more questions. Once they set out, he wasn't to talk. He was to wait for Haywire's hand signals.

"Krie, listen to whatever Uncle and I tell you because we will say it only once, so try to remember everything. This is bear and wolverine country. Learn to sense something behind you before you have to look. Bears hunt humans, and especially griz."

"HO!" came from outside the door.

"Uncle, thought you were still getting your beauty sleep!"

The door opened, and with it, a light feeling of happiness. A small man entered, with a rifle over one shoulder, and a pack on his back. He wore a green canvas coat and grey work pants. His smile lit the room. There were gaps where there should have been teeth, and his face was like crumpled paper. His brown skin glowed with health, and he walked over to Krie.

"You must be Krie."

"You must be Uncle."

"Uncle Angus."

"Hi, Uncle Angus, I'm happy to meet you. Haywire says you are the best hunter and trapper in the South Yukon."

"I don't know. Outfitters say different."

Krie forgot himself, "Outfitters?"

"Guiding outfits."

Krie learned that Uncle spoke in one- or two-word sentences a lot. He guessed that it was because extra words were not necessary when you are surrounded by bush, and always surrounded by your next possible meal.

"Ready?"

"Let's take it easy, this is Krie's first time."

"Okay." This, Krie would learn, was one of the three phrases Uncle used a lot.

"What do you think, Uncle?"

"Meadows."

"Signs there, then?"

"Yeah. Been rubbing the velvet off their horns."

Krie followed Haywire, who followed Uncle. Haywire turned to Krie once to motion to be quieter. Krie tried, but no matter what, his feet seemed to crush every stick, and blade of wild grass.

They walked on a narrow trail through mossy, tree-thick bush. The trees were small and narrow, and there were tiny trails everywhere. He thought they must be the game trails he had been hearing about. They stepped over a wide creek. Krie noticed the men became more vigilant. This was bear and wolverine country.

They caught an out of place sound long before they spotted the trucks. They came out onto a road, and Uncle made a low sound of disgust. There were two Hummers on the road and eight men dressed in camouflage were pointing huge rifles in the same direction.

Haywire said under his breath,

"Great."

The men did not notice them until they were a footfall behind them. Krie saw that they were aiming at the bush right beside a house. There was laughter in Haywire's voice.

"You trying to kill my mother?"

The men started, one whirled and pointed the gun at Haywire, who calmly reached out and pushed the barrel toward the ground.

"Shit, it's true; you Indians really *can* sneak up."

"Yeah, like everything you saw in a John Wayne movie is true."

"We saw a bear over there."

"Yeah? Was it wearin' a navy-blue coat?"

"No, we saw something moving around, it was big."

"Probably my Mother using the outhouse. Now lower those rifles before you shoot somebody."

"Your Mother?"

Just then a very large woman with very black hair, who looked just like Uncle, came out from behind the house.

"Ho," she called and nodded her head up. "Thought I was 'bout to meet my Waterloo!"

She broke out laughing, and Haywire said, "There's your grizzly, name's Doris."

The men in camo looked sheepish. Doris came over across the road. She was wearing bush clothes and a smile that looked just like Uncle's.

"Got time for tea?"

"Why, sure." Krie soon learned this was one of Uncle's other favourite phrases.

"You people come too before you shoot your feet off."

The men shuffled, one shrugged, and they put their guns in the trucks.

"Safe to leave these here?" Haywire had a quick retort waiting on his tongue.

"Not unless the squirrels need guns."

The men followed across the road, and all came into the little cabin. Krie walked into the outside porch and smelled bannock. His mouth watered.

There was nothing in the room but a large barrel stove, a countertop, and a table with benches. All the men crammed on them, and Doris put bannock, lard, salt, and a gigantic teapot and sugar on the table. There was only one spoon for the sugar, and she poured tea into mismatched mugs.

"What you boys lookin' for?" Angus was serious.

"Griz, mostly," said one, whose mouth was full of bannock. He took a big sip of tea and winced.

"Huh. I thought elephants, by the size of those guns of yours."

"You gonna have to climb for grizzlies," Haywire pitched in. "They'll be down for Bear Root pretty soon."

"Sonny, who are you?" Doris looked at Krie.

"I'm Krie." Her face froze. She glanced at Haywire quickly, then looked at the floor.

"He came to learn bush ways, Mom."

"*Nda!* Come with me," she up nodded to Krie, and motioned with her head to the other room.

Krie could hear the men asking Uncle about the area, about game; and he heard the respect in their voices.

"Am I to call you Auntie?"

"Sure, sonny, you call me Auntie Doris. Here, got something for you."

She pulled out a dresser drawer. Besides the bed, that was the one and only thing in the room.

"Aha!" Krie looked out the window and saw a burn pile, an outhouse, and a firepit.

"Here, *shashcho,* this was Arthur's when he was a sonny boy bout your size."

"Thanks, thanks so much." In his hand lay a knife in a leather sheath that was beautifully beaded with what looked to be wild roses. He turned it over and saw that it was beaded on the other side as well. There was a series of grizzly tracks, looking like they walked right of the case.

"Careful, sonny." Doris's voice was concerned when Krie undid the sheath and removed the knife.

"It's very sharp," she warned.

"This is a wonderful gift, thank you, *meegwitch!*"

"What lingo's that?"

"Oh, that's my Dad's language, and my Grandmother's."

"I see, well, around here we say *Gunatchish.*"

"*Gunalcheeshe,*" Krie attempted. Doris laughed and so did Krie.

"You'll get it yet, sonny boy."

Back in the kitchen, the hunters were curious about Uncle's and Haywire's guns. They seemed intrigued by the fact that all they used was .22 and .33 calibre rifles. They handled the guns with care and passed them around. Those guns looked old and Krie felt gratified when the large man said, "You sure take care of your firearms; these old beauties are in fantastic shape."

"These belonged to my Grandfather," was all Haywire said.

They all went out to the Hummers to see the equipment the hunters had.

Uncle whistled.

"Never seen stuff like this since the American Army came through here in the '40s."

Krie followed Haywire and Angus down the trail behind Doris's house. Haywire was behind him, Uncle in front. He knew it was for protection. He was carrying a .22 with what Haywire called ".22 shorts." He was given only one bullet. Haywire had said that it was all he should need. One chance, to take one sure shot, no wasted chances.

Krie strained his eyes, scanned everywhere, but could not see anything. Then, there it was, a reddish-brown showing between the trees. He held his breath, and then let it out. Haywire motioned to him to stay with Uncle and began moving across the meadow. Krie could tell by the hand signal Uncle had made that he was going to circle around in back of the animal.

Uncle was silent and seemed to be crouching on the balls of his feet; his whole being alert. Haywire made a wide arc and was moving like the wind, soundless, almost imperceptible. The animal must have been eating, its head was down most of the time. Each time its head came up, Haywire stopped a microsecond before. It was as if he knew exactly when the creature would move its head to look.

Uncle readied his .30-30. Krie watched as Angus and the gun became one, an extension of arms, eyes, intent. Something dropped near to the animal, and it started. It moved out into the meadow, did not run, but stood as if it knew its fate, and was submitting. It looked over, turned slightly, and to the side.

The shot crashed into the silence, and Krie jumped. The moose crashed to the ground and did not move. Haywire came out of the trees and walked to it. Krie thought he walked like he was part of the land. He tried to feel this as he and Uncle joined Haywire. Krie saw that Uncle's bullet had hit above and behind the left front leg. He was amazed at the size of the horns and the perfect, wild beauty of this animal.

Uncle said something to the moose in Tagish and then began cleaning it. Krie was fascinated by how quickly he opened and gutted the animal. The insides spilled out as if they had intent, and it was a release. They steamed in the cold air. It had a strange smell, but somehow a good one. Haywire reached in and cut something with his knife.

"Where's your salt. Krie?"

Krie quickly got it from his pack, curious. Haywire sprinkled salt on a piece of the innards and handed it to Krie.

"Eat this. Called 'the bible.'" Krie put it in his mouth. It had a strange texture but tasted good. He chewed and felt as though now he was part of this, part of the animal, part of the land, part of the hunt. Haywire instructed him to clean and gather up the guts.

"These we will take it back to Gramma Maisey; she will be very happy to have them for dinner."

Krie watched carefully as the skin fell away from the knife like the truth. The outside with thick short fur and the inside palest pink with only tiny bits of fat left. He was amazed at how deft Uncle was and how careful. Haywire pointed out the bladder and explained to Krie that under no circumstances must this ever be punctured, or it would spoil the meat. Uncle had not spoken until now, but added, "It is good to wait until you have one clear shot. This is the way I was taught. You wait for the animal to give itself, and never take a bad shot. The animal panics, and runs, and your meat will be tough, and full of the suffering. It is best to take the animal that gives itself. This meat is always full of goodness and tastes good. And it chews.

"How many European hunters have asked me how to tenderize meat? I always say, 'Shoot it the right way.' They never understand. If you respect animals, and take them right, with one shot, when they offer themselves, then the meat will always be tender."

The shadows were long by the time the moose was cut in pieces that could be hauled out. Haywire showed Krie how to strap the ribs to a pack board. Haywire and Uncle took a quarter each. Krie had the head and was surprised how heavy it was.

"We are going to haul this to the cabin and come back for the rest, so the animals and ravens don't get it."

The trip back was hard. Though they didn't walk through the buck-brush, they may as well have, the weight of his pack pushed Krie so close to the earth that he tripped numerous times. Haywire turned to make the quiet sign more than once. Finally, he turned and said,

"Find the eyes in your feet again. It's different with the weight, just focus on looking ahead and being aware of what's around you. If there are bears or wolves, they will be attracted to the smell of fresh game."

Krie did as he was told. It was like the meditation he was taught in public school the year before. Soon they were back at the cabin. When the meat was stowed in the cache, they set out right away after a quick drink of water from the eddy near the cabin. The water tasted delicious, and Krie had never felt his thirst so quenched. They set off in twilight, and Krie did not trip this time. Haywire turned to smile. Krie's heart soared. He did not know why it felt so important to please Haywire, but it made him feel happy inside. They reached the site, Haywire gave Krie the guts. The remaining two quarters and ribs were taken by Haywire and Uncle. For an old man, he was very strong, Krie thought, as he watched Uncle walk, straight-backed, at the same speed as when they were coming back from the cabin. It was dark, and nobody used a light. Uncle seemed to know this place like the land right around the cabin, as did Haywire. Krie realized that if you saw with your feet, then it was like any other place, your "foot eyes" would remember the dips and mounds. He tried to remember. They were taking a different route this time. He did not ask questions. He had already been told that in the bush you spoke only when necessary. After a time, he saw lights twinkling through the trees ahead. They came out of the woods to a newer house, with dim light spilling out of the windows in a gold red glow.

Uncle called out, "Mom, get water, got guts."

Krie heard an older lady laughing within as the door opened,

"Good, good, come in." Her voice happy.

He saw the oldest face he had ever seen, on a tiny older lady. She was drawing water from a pail into a huge basin. Haywire said,

"Gramma, this is my pardner Krie; Krie, this is Gramma Maisey Charlie."

"Hello."

"Hello."

"Put 'em here."

Krie watched as Gramma Maisey cleaned the contents of the guts into one basin, then placed them in the basin with water and deftly washed them clean. Haywire motioned to Krie to build up the stove. He set to work outside cutting wood carefully and learning to use night eyes. He came back with an armload of kindling and filled the bin. Then he returned with split wood. He split a number of logs and piled them carefully near the door. When he came in, he carefully built the fire on the coals that glowed inside the stove. He looked around. Like Doris's place, this one was sparse. A kitchen counter, a stove in the corner, a water barrel, a table and chairs. One easy chair by the window. Beneath his feet, Krie saw the same plain lino tile. Gramma walked awkwardly over to Krie.

"Who you?"

"I'm Krie."

"You like moose guts?"

"Never had them."

"Ho, real good. You gonna like it." With her dialect good sounded like "goot."

Gramma Maisey was tiny but took up presence in the room like a circus barker. Krie knew that she was kind but tough. He could tell by the glint in her eye that she was feisty and liked to laugh. Gramma Maisey set him to work cutting up the long tubes that were called "bum guts." She built up the stove, and put a cast-iron frypan on the top, with a large pot of boiling water.

"Some people, they like it boiled – me, I like it fried."

It was delicious. Krie felt the energy of this meal surge through him.

It was late enough by the time the three of them safely stowed the rest of the meat in the cache. Krie loved how the cache looked like a tiny log cabin on stilts. He had to scramble up a ladder to get in, which was hard on the body, carrying weight. His muscles ached, and he was bone tired. Haywire must have noticed.

That night, everyone heard the rapping at the windows. It was a feeling that iced your insides. Nobody acknowledged or moved from their beds, but everyone heard it. At the door, a window, the window on the opposite side of the little house, then the other. On the stovepipe. All night Bonewalker spoke to them with those tappings. Not one of them slept. Krie knew that it could not get in, or it would not be making noise. It did not help him to feel better. It was almost worse to hear that tap-tap-tapping. He could not help himself but kept straining to hear, which in this silence was an easy thing. It was a dreading of the next sound and the cold terror that stole around his entire being like a blanket of frost. He kept willing it to know that he would fight.

"You will not win" he told Bonewalker over and over.

"You will go to the in-between, and I will make you."

"I am stronger, and I walk in the light."

He willed love into his heart. It pushed the fear out, but it kept sneaking back in the door. He knew this was part of the game. It was so hard to put the love back, but all night he did this. He thought of Auntie, of Grandmother, and he thought of his real Mother. He had them in a circle around him. When he did sleep, the Bonewalker leered at him from outside.

"Your Mother's crazy, and you will be, too. You can't get away from me. Nobody is strong enough. I *will* get you."

In the morning, Uncle and Gramma Maisey talked quietly in the corner. Uncle was at the table with Haywire when Krie woke up from a doze. Uncle was watching him, but not with his eyes. Krie stretched.

"Young pup, come and have bannock and tea."

"*Nu-h*," he said as he passed him a cup and plate.

Krie saw someone had fried fresh meat. He put lard and salt on his bannock the way he had seen the others do it. On top, he placed a chunk of meat. It was delicious. He put sugar in his tea and enjoyed the heat of it in the cool of the morning. Uncle had something, and he wasn't saying much. He held the thing in his hand, and Krie felt his mood; it was serious. He was getting used to how quiet people stayed here. It was a comfortable quiet, that you could just be in, like a cool swim in summer, it was something to enjoy. It wasn't really quiet, there were things going on. He could feel each of them in the room enjoying one another. There was the sense of togetherness, peace. When he was finished, Uncle motioned for him to stand. He had something on a leather thong. He put it around Krie's neck. He looked him straight in the eyes. His eyes were full of love, and concern.

"Never take this off."

"I won't, Uncle."

"It's gonna help you."

"How, Uncle?"

"I'll teach you."

When he came down to the old Charlie cabin the next morning Angus announced the fish were running in the creek, it was gaffing time. Haywire glanced at the sky and downed the last bit of his coffee. Krie was ready before they gave him the word.

"Keep your back eyes on, bears and wolverines around."

Krie nodded and "turned on his senses." They walked up the narrow trail away from the lake and toward Doris's cabin. Again, he was in the middle, carrying a long pole, with a huge fish-hook-looking thing on the end of a long pole with three prongs. Uncle and Haywire carried their rifles. They walked through muskeg and trees that were small with gold leaves. Krie loved the little game trails that told stories about little animals. He could hear the water before he saw it.

The creek was wide enough to hop over, and Krie joined Uncle on the far side. There was one gaff hook. He watched as Uncle sharply forced it into the water and pulled it out with fish on it. Uncle passed it to Haywire after a time.

"Need a smoke." Haywire went to work, and it was not long before the bin was full of fish. The pole was passed to Krie. He straddled the creek and darted the pole in the water. A fish was splaying on the end like a dancer to and fro. He dropped it into the bucket. He kept going, getting into the rhythm with his breath, the pole, and the fish on the end, each time thanking the fish that had given themselves. He did not see Haywire and Uncle glance at each other and smile.

"It's full." He was learning to keep his voice low and phrases short.

The three of them shared the weight of the bin. At the cabin, they moved toward the little eddy where the boats were kept. Boards were fetched from the cabin, and Krie used his new knife to clean the fish.

"Need a fish knife – gotta keep that sharp for your first moose."

"I'll use it for now, Uncle." Krie was smiling.

The three cleaned fish, and Krie watched quickly to get the hang of it. When their boards were full of heads and guts, they would take them carefully to the water and respectfully release the guts to the lake. Krie knew this was a spiritual practice, just as whatever was not used from the moose had been carried to beneath a tree. He knew that water creatures went to the water, and land animals' remains went on the land. This was part of the respect for the animal's sacrifice.

That whole day was spent butchering at a huge table made out of a sheet of plywood and two sawhorses that materialized out of nowhere. Krie had helped fix the smoker, which was near the lake. The smoker was a series of poles set wide apart deep in the ground with more poles attached running horizontally, from the tops to a couple of feet from the bottom. A fire was built in the centre of the series of racks, and huge plastic pulled over the whole structure.

Once Doris had checked the condition of the plastic, it was taken off and laid on the wild grass. Then, two to a side, they all sliced meat in an assembly line. Uncle cut up the huge chunks, Haywire made them smaller still, and Doris and Krie sliced them over and over as thin as they could without perforating through. Doris showed him how to hang these on the racks. The fire was made with fresh-cut wood that smoked more than the inside fire. Some of the meat was cut in what looked like nunchuks. All was carefully laid over the drying racks, starting at the top, and then to the bottom. When they were full, the plastic was carefully pulled over the entire thing.

"You're gonna keep this fire smoky." Krie nodded.

"It's gonna smoke the meat, flavour it, and keep the flies off. We can eat it all winter. Back in my Dad and Mom's day, they sometimes smoke-dried most of a moose to make it easier to haul out. Back then, even the kids worked really hard."

"Mom is really wanting some birds, Angus."

"Oh?"

"Yeah, she was telling me this morning."

"Okay."

"Krie, pack up, we're headin' her in."

Krie smelled the animal before he saw it. He stayed quiet and saw both Uncle and Haywire freeze. Haywire made the sign for "stop" although Krie had already. They waited, motionless. There was nothing but the sound of the chatting leaves in the trees. Krie did not know how long they stood still but even though he needed to shift his weight, he resisted. He noted which way the wind was going and realized they were down-wind of whatever this was, and so were going to have to wait until the creature moved. He knew they weren't hunting it, because of the way Haywire and Uncle were looking. They held themselves as if they were alert and ready, but it was not the same feeling as when they were going to take down the moose. This was different. This was a wariness.

Krie focused on the feeling of the silence, the breeze playing across his face, the faint sun on his skin. He sensed the seasonal cool, and then the life all around him. He felt everything quietly growing, the trees, the grass, all that was around him. He felt animals moving about, and tiny insects on the ground. Uncle relaxed and made the okay sign. Krie made the sign for "what?"

Haywire signed back "wolverine." Krie knew that Haywire and Uncle had a respect for wolverines. Although they were not dangerous unless cornered, he has heard them speak of giving the animals a lot of room. The same with grizzlies. Krie knew they were both territorial, and that it was a delicate thing walking about in what they felt was their home. Something pulled his eyes left. There was an ugly sense, and he dreaded what he would see. It was Dale Post, peering from behind a tree.

He came to on the ground. Haywire and Uncle were bending over him.

"What happened?"

"Dale Post – he was right over there in those trees."

Haywire and Uncle looked at each other.

"Do you want to go back to the cabin?"

"No, Auntie Doris wants rabbit, let's go and find her some."

They set off again. The men did not ask him how he was after that. Krie realized that they trusted him to say if he needed to go back. It was something, having that kind of trust from adults. Mother and Grandmother would have made him go home no matter what. I guess this was how men were different. They expected you to be honest about going on. He hoped that he was going to be alright and did not want to force someone to have to take him back. He focused on the eyes in his feet and the eyes in his back. Uncle made the "stop, wait" sign. He turned slowly and pointed to a tree. Krie saw it. A grouse. Uncle motioned for him to take a shot. Krie slowly swung the rifle off his shoulder and loaded a shell. He pointed, sighted, breathed in, breathed out, sighted, and shot. The grouse dropped like a stone. His heart flew. He got it! Uncle only quietly said, "Good," but Krie was full of excitement as if he had done something huge. Haywire patted his shoulder.

"Let's go take care of it." Then, "Do you want to eat it now, or later?"

"Let's take it to Gramma Maisey."

Haywire nodded, and Krie could sense his pleasure, although he did not show it. "Okay, well, let's do her a favour and pluck it, then, it's harder when it's cold."

Krie felt the satisfying weight in his pack. Even Dale Post could not take away the glow that radiated from his chest now.

◉◉◉

"He's 13, Haywire, you can't do anything if the boy doesn't come home." Doris was serious, Angus nodded. Haywire gripped his tea, and the firelight played with the shadows on his face. The lines were carved deep, he looked old and tired.

"You have to let him make his own mistakes."

"I just worry about that Bonewalker."

"We all do."

Krie was numb all over. The alcohol made him feel alive and free. That girl he liked from the school was flirting with him across the room where she giggled with her friends. Now he had the courage, he called out across the noise of the party.

"Tina, come sit with me."

She giggled and smiled in a way no 13-year-old girl should know how to smile, sashayed across the room. It was like she came in slow motion. He knew every guy was watching her. The music sounded far away, and as if it was underwater, but the drumbeat was steady and loud, echoing like a heartbeat. She sat right on his lap. This girl who he had been afraid to talk to in class. He felt no awkwardness now, no hesitation.

"I like you."

"I like you; you aren't the same as the others."

"I shouldn't be."

"How about you and I go in the bedroom?"

"Why?"

"Why do you think, silly?"

This was not what he wanted. What he wanted was to tell her he loved her and that he wanted to be with her. But she was pulling him through the crowd of people; some passed out on the floor already. Two boys were starting to fight. She led him around them and into a back room. He felt a little sick. She pulled him to the filthy bed, where she lay down and pulled him beside her. She began kissing him. When her tongue entered his mouth, he tasted the liquor on her and jumped. He was overcome with a wave of longing, heat and wanted to touch her all over. He wanted her. His head swam with confusion. This was not right. She was too young. He was too young, but it felt as though his body had a mind of its own, and so did his heart. He could not fight. Then she froze.

"The fuck is that old guy?"

"What?"

"Who the fuck is that creepy old guy watching us?"

He sat up, fighting the spinning of the world. Dale Post stood in the corner of the room. Krie spewed.

"Oh, God, gross!" Tina got up and left the room, and he knew that was it. But it didn't matter. Dale Post was leering and taunting when he put his head back and laughed a terrible rattling laugh. It was a triumphant and ugly sound. Krie stood, fought his way outside, threw up again, lay on the cool earth, and tried like hell not to be drunk. Bonewalker followed, crawling behind, snickering until Krie crawled in the yard with the dogs. Bonewalker could not go there or the dogs would howl. He was very angry. He should have taken his chance while the soul was numbed by the drink.

Krie woke up someplace he did not recognize. A couple of old Grannies were watching him from a table in the corner where there was tea. They weren't looking at him, but he felt their other eyes on him.

"Little sick there, sonny?"

"Yeah. My head feels like it's a hollow rock filled with cotton candy. My stomach feels like it hates me."

"It does, my boy," said the eldest. With a sinking stomach, he recognized Gramma Fran, Uncle Angus' sister.

"*Nu-h*. Tea and bannock here. Keep it down, you be better."

"How did I get here?"

"You just walked in."

"Yep, 2 o'clock in the mornin' jes like you live here. Dogs told us you were comin'."

He had a faint recollection of a symphony of barking dogs the night before and the sense of needing a safe place.

"Sorry, Grammas, sorry." He put his head down and sighed.

"We know; you said."

"This is my young sister Bess," Gramma Fran motioned to the other.

"Who is 'Bastard Post?'" Gramma Bess was curious.

"My Father."

"That's no way to call your Father."

"I know, sorry, Grammas."

"Best get you back to Little Annie."

He groaned. He had forgotten he was still in Carcross. Memories of the night before walked rudely through the door of his mind, unwanted. How would he face Haywire and Uncle? His stomach rose in his throat. He ran out the door and threw up in the yard. He retched and retched, but nothing was there to come out.

"Tea and bannock, now," said Fran.

It was the hardest thing he had ever done but he forced it all down his throat, which rebelled and tried to bring it back up.

"We drive you home, okay?"

The cold air felt good on his face. It chilled his skin, and he felt better now. These two grannies were gentle with him, unjudging. He did not see a vehicle. He looked around and did not see a garage. What he did see were a lot of raggedy dogs, tied up over the yard. Bess hauled a sleigh from behind the house. *"You gotta be kiddin',"* he thought. He watched with growing admiration as the two Elders began harnessing all the dogs together. The dogs were acting crazy; stamping, jumping, whining, yipping, barking, like they were dying to get going and pull. The Grammas talked to each one as they hooked them in. The younger one came around the side of the house with a bucket, threw a fish to each dog, who snapped it in waiting jaws and devoured it in seconds.

"Okay, sonny, climb on, get you home in no time." He climbed on the sleigh and was surprised when the two old ladies did not. The dogs did not need to be told, but took off, running and barking, and yipping. Their breath rose in the cold air, and Krie settled in the sleigh. He turned around to see Gramma Bess on the runners, and Gramma Fran running behind! They crossed the lake, and Krie looked up to the mountains. They were touched with the gold of the morning sun against the clear and cloudless sky. He felt peace, as though this was the only place to be on the whole earth. He turned to watch Gramma Fran who was still running. She wasn't even panting. They went "full throttle" all the way, as Haywire would say. They avoided the roads, and instead took well-worn trails through the bush. His stomach felt better, and his headache receded. The rhythmic movement of the dogs was meditative, and Krie felt elated. He turned to the two Grammas and shouted: "I don't know why people have snowmobiles; this is AWESOME!"!

Gramma Bess snorted. "Say that when you gotta get up at 5 every day and cook the dog feed!" Krie turned and grinned, and she grinned back. Gramma Fran was still not panting! They crossed over the Tagish bridge. Krie craned his neck to look up and then downriver. Nobody was around, but the beauty around him made him think of a postcard. It was still, pristine. In that perfect tranquility a Bonewalker was running behind.

When they stopped, the dogs were cavorting, twisting, and yipping in their harnesses. Clouds of steam rose from their bodies. Their hot breath slowly rose in the cold in tiny clouds. The ladies came with Krie to the door. They were met by Uncle, who, smiling broadly, waved them in for tea. Krie's head hung low. Haywire looked up from where he was working on a stretcher.

"Good of you to bring home the lost pup."

"Couldn't have him around that long, got all those other pups to feed."

"Thanks, we were worried."

Krie's neck reddened.

"Ahhh, he was no trouble. Jes' walked in my shack like he owned it is all," said Gramma Bess, laughter in her voice. Krie felt sicker.

"Nothin' worse than you done not too long ago, you two"! Gramma Maisey motioned toward Uncle and Haywire.

"Krie, haul some water and wood." Haywire's voice had a little hardness.

"Ok." He felt like hell. He did the chores, and though it made him feel a little weak, the exertion actually settled him. He started to breathe deeply, and the hangover began to recede.

"Right on track." Through the open door, he heard a harsh laugh from beyond the trees.

"Fuck you," he replied to the Bonewalker, without looking up.

When he stepped in, Haywire's voice reached him at the door.

"Put that down and come with me."

He followed Haywire up the old dirt track used for vehicles. He stopped on the little hill and hesitated. Krie followed him to the little family graveyard. There were more graves than Krie had seen passing from the road. Each had a little fence around it; one had a little shed with windows. He walked up to that one.

"This is my Grandfather Tom, Gramma Maisey's husband. This is my Uncle Charlie, and this is Uncle Wilfred. Auntie Minnie, Auntie Jessie, Auntie Clara. Three babies Gramma and Grampa Charlie had that didn't make it, so were not named. In all, Gramma and Grampa had 18."

Krie saw the remnants of objects that had been placed on the graves sticking out of the snow. And this, he stopped in front of a small grave on which there was a little baby doll's arm sticking out of the snow. It was eerie.

"This is your older sister, Laya."

Krie felt as if he had been gut-punched.

"She died at birth, out in the meadows. Your Mom hid the pregnancy. She and I were not sleeping in the same room or getting along. I thought she was cheating on me. Nobody knew. Your Mom went off in the meadows and the baby was stillborn. My Uncle found your Mom. He either knew or she told him it was Dale Post's baby. They buried it there, but I moved her here to be with the family."

Krie could not help the tears that streamed down his face. He stayed silent.

You had a brother. We don't know what happened, but he was kidnapped by Post. He disappeared. Krie began to sob.

"I know where he is."

"You can choose to let pain rule your life, use it as an excuse to drink, to hurt yourself or others. I did. I drank when I thought your Mom was cheating, and I hurt her badly, and myself, and my family."

Krie felt shame creep inside and a sadness for his brother.

"Stop that guilt; it is the thing that drives the wheel."

"What wheel?"

"Of addiction. Shame drives it, makes you feel so bad you want to numb out again. It's a wasted feeling. Stop."

Krie nodded. He felt like hell.

"I'm sorry I let you and Uncle down."

"You let yourself down."

"I know. I know."

"You have to be stronger than the troubles you have to face. You have to know that pain is just life's way of telling you something is wrong. You just have to sit with it and figure out what it's trying to tell you."

"Ok, I will."

"Your Mom used to say that it was like a ring of fire. She knew she had to go in there. She was not going to run around in it screaming about how it hurt; and she wasn't going to stay there. She said she ran in, looked for the gift, grabbed it, and booked it out the other side. She said the gift was the thing, not the pain. So Krie, look for the gift."

"Mom couldn't bear the last gift."

"She will, the gift was you."

He waved the ladies off down the trail. He listened as the barking and yapping retreated into the distance. He finally walked into the cabin, hauling the water pail so as not to spill then went back out for the wood and loaded much more than he needed to into the pile beside the stove. Uncle and Haywire were quiet.

"Just gonna hand yourself over to that Bonewalker, then?"

"I was stupid".

Uncle laughed.

"They make you stupid? Those you walk away from."

"I know. I just had to do something really dumb to figure that out."

"Well, how you feel is punishment enough."

"Put gas in the Ski-Doo, settin' traps today." Krie wanted to groan out loud but did not. Uncle and Haywire winked at each other. Krie did not see them but felt it.

They were on foot. Krie knew the pace was slower because of him and felt like a fool. Would he ever get it right? He wanted so much to make these men proud of him, and he had done the worst thing ever. How could he ever make it up? He was disgusted with himself. Uncle swung around on the trail to face him. He was serious.

"Stop!" His voice was low.

"You are *here* now. Not back in town. Put that behind you."

Krie felt humbled and small. How had Uncle known?

He turned on his bush senses and focused on where he was. Haywire turned to smile. How had he known? Haywire winked and grinned widely. It was much cooler, and the ground felt hard under his feet. Krie had been so occupied in the past week that he had not noticed. He chided himself. Haywire turned; his face serious. Krie got the message. "*Man. These two miss nothing.*" He willed himself away from those thoughts and back to the present. He smelled the freezing air; it was already freezing the nose hairs. It had to be close to zero. The fall scents had disappeared with the coming of the frost. The ground was uneven and had no give. Frost coated every-thing, each blade of grass, each twig.

They walked until Uncle made the sign for "here." Hay-wire motioned for Krie to get water. The creek was still run-ning. He took the coffee can from Uncle's outstretched hand, straddled the stream and dipped, careful not to spill. He knew even that would alert any game. He carried it to where Haywire was making a tiny fire. Uncle motioned "cold" and "tea." Krie was glad. He needed warming. Krie took teabags and sugar from his pack. He watched the steaming water, heard the hiss of droplets on the side in the flames. At the moment it boiled, he tossed teabags and sugar in. Haywire used a stick to lift the makeshift handle up, picked up the can carefully, moving it aside.

The tea steamed like breath clouds as it was poured, and they all squatted, blowing their cups until it was cooled enough. He felt the conversation that was within the silence. If he was present within that silence, he felt it. He looked up. Haywire was smiling slightly, stirring the coals. He motioned only with his eyes to the creek, and very quickly, without moving his head. Krie got it, rising with the tin, and going for more water. He did not see Uncle and Haywire grin at each other. He felt it, though. He understood now. This was the key to staying within the moment. It was to hear with inner ears, just like he saw with the eyes in his feet and back. This was another world.

Bonewalker watched from a distance from the trees. He could not come closer when the child was in a state of awareness. He was angry. It had been so close, especially when the child had taken the alcohol. This was going to be much more difficult than he thought, but he liked a challenge. It was so much more satisfying to win. He hunkered down for the wait; there was no point in following.

Uncle stopped just as Krie's stomach was demanding food. Haywire silently pointed out a rabbit that was crouched, still, not far from where they were. Haywire shouldered his .22 and shot. The animal flopped on its side. Haywire skinned the rabbit, and soon it was on a stick resting across two forked sticks, and over the fire. The grease from the rabbit dripped and hissed into the flames, and the aroma had Krie feeling absolutely ready to eat anything by the time it was ready. Haywire gently pulled a leg off and handed it to Krie. He motioned to wait, and Krie blew on the steaming, dripping meat. He bit in feeling the heat between his teeth.

Rabbit was like chicken, but not completely. It was tougher, and had a wild taste, but he loved it, and the juice that ran down his chin. Krie rose without being asked and used his nose to locate the creek. He filled the coffee can and went back. He found a handful of coffee in his pack, and it floated on the water. Krie remembered the cold-water trick and set off toward the creek. He dipped his mug in and filled it halfway. He drank the sweet, cold water. It tasted of all the beauty in the meadow, of flowers, and pure air full of everything growing around him. Krie dipped again and savoured the cold liquid that seemed to taste of every flower, and every plant growing nearby. He dipped once more, watching the droplets off his cup land in the creek.

Now Krie made his way back and saw another rabbit. Carefully putting his mug down, he swung his .22 from off his shoulder and clicked off the safety. Krie loaded, and quietly using the bolt, clicked the shell into the chamber. He took his time. Krie aimed, waited, held his breath, and fired. The crack seemed loud in the air. He walked to the animal and thanked it. Krie took it by the ears as he had seen Haywire do.

When he reached the fire, he gently laid the rabbit near Haywire. Krie saw the coffee was coming to a boil, so poured the cold water on the top. The grounds sank. He reached to take the can off the fire and placed it on a rock. When Krie looked up the other men were smiling. He skinned the rabbit as he had seen Haywire do. Krie could feel their pride in him, and he revelled in their satisfaction. Krie carefully placed the rabbit in his pack, so the two would know it wasn't going to be cooked. Krie had a glow in his middle that nothing could take away, or so he thought.

◉◉◉

Trap setting was not hard work, but it meant a long day. Each trap had to be baited, hidden. Krie learned that this took infinite patience, like most bush work Angus and Haywire worked together like an old team. Angus motioned to Krie that the handling of the traps was always with gloves on, so human scent was not left on the metal. Different bait was used for each animal being trapped. For beaver no bait, but careful placing of traps on their trails. Krie remembered seeing "ban leg-hold traps" on a bumper sticker down south. He thought at this moment that it was a bigger thing than that – this, he knew, was the winter survival for Tlingit-Tagish people, and had been for as long as non-Indian people had come to this land. It was just not that simple. It was work, just like any other, supply and demand. And people South would not understand the balance of nature that Tlingit-Tagish people did. Oh. Clear the mind, he thought. I am thinking again. Haywire glanced up at him with a smile. Krie moved to find small sticks and tufts of dried grass for Haywire to hide the traps.

The sun was low in the sky, a dark gold, and the shadows were long when they headed for home.

Doris was almost ecstatic when Krie delivered the rabbit to her on the way home.

"You fellas want to help me eat this feast?" They said nothing, but relaxed in chairs, and Haywire and Uncle rolled smokes. They did not smoke when they were out; Krie realized any strange odour would scare game. Krie followed Doris out to see how she cleaned the rabbit. It was quick. She cut at the feet and neck, held the ears and peeled the fur inside out – like peeling pajamas off a kid. When it was skinned, he was surprised that it was the size of a roasting chicken.

That night, as Krie lay in his bed, a feeling of strangeness came over him. He was aware of nothing until he woke in the dark, with the sense of being held to the cot by a heavy weight. He heard a cackling in his ear. His stomach lurched in fear, and his body tensed. He felt the strong urge to urinate, and his bowels felt loose. The horrid breath was in his face.

"Bastard," the Bonewalker hissed in his ear, but Krie was in Grandmother's embrace, and he could feel her arms around him, hear her voice.

"Sing your song, Krie."

He sang as if his life depended on it. He sang his heart out, for Grandmother, for Mother, for Leah, and for all of them. His voice filled the cabin. Haywire and Uncle woke and lay still. This fight, they knew, was the child's. Haywire stilled himself and listened to the song. Uncle prayed. Haywire heard him move, and knew he was reaching for his tobacco. It was a long time before Krie stopped. There was nothing, then, but the crackle of the fire in the stove. And peace.

In the morning, Krie was up early, and had hauled water and made a fire before the others had woken. He had the coffee on when Haywire got up to use the outhouse.

"Good morning. Had yourself a little sing-song last night?"

"The Bonewalker got in here."

"You can take bannock and some of the dry meat for lunch."

"That's my favorite, but I have to hide it from the town kids."

Haywire laughed.

"I remember the same thing when I had to go back to Mission School. The kids would beg me for it like it was candy."

"That must have been hard, Haywire."

"Nah. I took extra, hid it under my clothes, so I could share."

"No, I mean Mission School."

"I am just glad it closed down. I'm glad you'll never have to live through that."

"Me too, Haywire. I'm sorry you had to."

"It made me who I am. It made me love our way of life."

"It got to him the other night, in a dream."

"Dreams is okay that doesn't mean he isn't protected; it means he's gifted." Uncle sighed and relaxed, nodding.

"The fight, it's going to be a big one. I can't see if he will win. I only know he is strong. We just got to pray. And bring him! Oh. And you tell him, be careful. That medicine the Bonewalker cannot cross. One time someone did that medicine, and they didn't know the Bonewalker was still inside. They trapped it inside their house, and that's how it eventually got them."

The sun was low in the sky. When the truck stopped at the cabin, Uncle said only,

"Gonna run the traps." Haywire nodded. He knew Uncle would be out there praying for Krie in his own way.

It was sundown before Angus returned, and Krie was already home enjoying a snack. Angus did not have his pack on.

"What did we get, Uncle?"

"Boot up; come see."

Krie and Haywire joined Angus where he was detaching something from his pack board. Krie saw a large animal with thick fur.

"Lynx!"

"Yep, and a big healthy one, too." Angus's voice was light. Krie knew this was going to bring enough money to feed them for at least a month.

"Can I help, Uncle?"

"Why, sure!" This meant Uncle was happy he asked. Krie grinned. He ran back to the cabin for his knife.

The silence was broken by a vehicle. Haywire and Angus looked at each other. Krie stood looking at them.

Krie asked no questions. He didn't wonder why Haywire had never mentioned a family. Maybe it was too hard to talk about. Haywire looked tired when he came in. Uncle was all smiles and started teaching them counting in the language. (One, Two, Three). Uncle was cheery.

"You boys want to help me skin a Lynx?" They nodded and got busy getting boots and coats on.

"Wonder when the last time they ate was," Haywire said mostly to himself. "Woman never takes care of those boys right." Krie said nothing.

"Ah," he said in disgust. "They'll ask when they're hungry."

Krie could feel the dark mood that had crept over Haywire. It was unlike him. There was a story here.

"Dar runs off. We have a house in Tagish. It's just too hard to be there when the boys are gone." Krie nodded. He sensed if he stayed silent, Haywire would answer his questions.

"She got pregnant, that's why I am with her. Dar is a party girl. No amount of kids is gonna change that. I try to be there for the kids. She isn't much of a Mother. More interested in what guy can supply her with beer and sex until she is tired of them, or the money runs out. They're good boys, but they seen way too much. I can't get custody because of my past. She's stayed off the radar, it's hard for those boys. I'll set her up at the house tomorrow, and we will be moving there with the boys. At least until she takes off. It will be a couple of weeks at most before she's gone. You understand, right?"

Krie was careful with his words. He could feel how hard this was for Haywire.

"Whatever we have to do for the boys, I'm in."

Haywire smiled gently at Krie.

"You're a good kid," was all he replied.

Krie set to work making supper. When it was done, he called the boys in. There were only three plates, so he would wash theirs when they were done. Billy and Ronnie stormed in the door, with all the energy that excited little boys bring in with the frigid air.

"Come eat."

"What is it? It smells so good, not like baloney samwich."

"Moose stew and bannock."

The boys ate like they had not eaten for days. Krie gave them three plates each before they were done. Haywire came from the back room.

"Okay, boys, time to get some sleep. Come and I will tell you a story, okay?"

"We missed you, Daddy." Ronnie's little voice was as soft and pathetic as a kitten's mew.

"Yeah, nobody else EVER tells us stories."

The door opened. "That hide will need working; I'll show you tomorrow. Oh. That's right. Well, I'll show you when you come on the weekend. Teach you how to stretch furs."

"Sounds good, Uncle. Come have your stew."

Uncle was quiet as he ate.

"You give them boys lots of love, ok Krie? Not their fault how their Mom is. Teach them everything I've taught you."

"You aren't going anywhere, are you?"

"No, but you will be in Tagish mostly. It'll help 'em, and you for you to teach 'em. It's an old way we love little ones."

Krie was thoughtful.

"Saturday, we be taking the lot of you to visit Gramma Maisey." Krie nodded.

"You all be needin' her help."

Krie didn't like Tagish. It was beautiful alright, with the river running through and the mountains all around, but it wasn't Little Annie. He already missed the cabin and Uncle. He and Haywire had driven the road between Little Annie and Tagish in silence. Haywire turned the truck off in front of a little house by the river. He hesitated, taking a firm grip on the steering wheel.

"We live with our mistakes ,Krie. We're free to make decisions, but never free from the cost." He grabbed his smokes, and his duffle from behind the seat.

"Lemme get this over with. Take the boys to the river; it's never a happy reunion." Krie nodded.

"I need the bathroom first."

His stomach was tight. He knew he was picking up on Haywire, and he also knew that they while they were doing the right thing,that living here was not going to be comfortable.

Darlene looked up when Haywire entered, Krie behind him. She was on the couch, lighting a fresh smoke. Her hands trembled. Krie knew it wasn't fear.

"This is Krie, Dar, he will be staying with us."

Darlene did not greet Krie or look up.

"Got the smokes and money?"

"Yeah, here. Gonna cut some wood."

"Need the truck, headin' to Carcross for food."

"I brought groceries. It's all in the back of the truck."

Darlene's face darkened with a red flush.

"I needed to visit Auntie, too."

"I guess you haven't heard; your Auntie's been in hospital in Whitehorse for months; she had a stroke."

Darlene said nothing but threw the TV remote into the corner.

"I know you want beer. It's in the truck, too."

"Well, why didn't you say so!"

Krie was getting the boys re-coated and re-booted. The air was live with Darlene's hostility; an electrical current snapping, crackling, between her and Haywire. Krie spoke up.

"Haywire, me and the boys will unload after our walk." He knew it was more medicine than beer and that Darlene was "drunk sick." He had heard kids at school talk about how some people used it each day to keep the "detox sicks" at bay. Krie felt sorry for Darlene. At that moment she shot him a look. It was then he understood that she was angry and sick, but not without gifts. There is more to her than meets the eye, he thought. He swore he saw a little smile curl at the side of her mouth.

"We can't go near the water," Billy said.

"Yeah, some other little kid drownded."

Krie took them down the path that led from the bridge downriver.

"You got your foot eyes on?" The boys laughed.

"We don't have eyes in our feet!" Ronnie said. They were both giggling.

"Well, if you are going to walk in the bush, you will need them, then you can look forward and not down. You won't trip."

"You got your back eyes on?"

"We don't got back eyes," the boys said together, giggling harder.

"Yeah, you got to turn those on, too, in the bush, so nothing sneaks up on you." The boys were busy grabbing sticks and rocks out of the snow. Their happy chattering did not drown out Darlene's angry voice coming down the river from the house.

Things were quiet until the boys crashed through the door of the house. It was an uneasy silence, not a peaceful one. Like a silence after the storm where wreckage needs to be surveyed.

"You boys, put your coats and boots back in the mud room," Darlene yelled from the kitchen.

Haywire was nowhere to be seen. Darlene was dishing out supper.

She looked up at Krie.

"You're that Leah's boy, aren't you?" He nodded.

"That woman has been the ghost in my life."

"I don't understand."

"How could you? Haywire has always loved her. Never loved me. I know that. I might not act like it, but I have always loved him. He just doesn't see me. He is blinded by your Mom. When he looks at me, he is seeing what I'm not. I can never live up to her, can never be enough." Krie saw the tears before she turned away.

"I'm not a bad person. I just go 'cause I can't stand it any-more. I try to get his attention by taking the boys and leaving, and he just lets me go, doesn't care. I hate him, and I love him. Hate him for wanting me to be someone else, for looking at me like I am always going to not be her. And I love him because, well, because he is Haywire." Her shoulders were heaving. The boys, oblivious, were excitedly finding toys as if they were old friends as they emptied a big chest in the living room off the kitchen.

"You look like you need a hug." She clung to Krie like a bear cub and sobbed. Haywire's voice came low from where he was standing in the doorway.

"Not going after the 13-year-old now, are you?"

He ducked when the spatula flew past his head. Krie felt sick to his stomach.

The next morning, Krie and Haywire were having coffee.

"You know, Darlene really loves you, Haywire."

"Don't even know if those boys are mine."

"They both look just like you."

"I care for them, because someone has to."

"She loves you, Haywire. She was crying last night; I was hugging her because she was really hurting."

"I don't know that the woman has feelings. Be careful of her, Krie. She's trouble."

"She really was sad. I could feel it in my belly."

"Just be careful, son."

The days had lengthened. It felt weird to leave in the dark and get home in the dark.

When he closed the door, the boys ran to him and jumped all around like puppies. Laughing, he rolled to the floor and wrestled them around for a few minutes. Darlene smiled down at the three of them. She was actually very pretty when she smiled. She lit a new smoke, and blew a long, luxurious trail as she exhaled.

"Where's Haywire?" Krie was curious, but also felt a little uncomfortable being alone with Darlene after the conversation with Haywire.

"Store."

"There's a store?" Krie was amazed. She laughed.

"About all there is."

She looked up when Haywire entered, and her face changed, serious.

"Dar, here's that tea you like. The store got some in, I bought the whole case." Darlene's face softened.

"You bought this for me?" Haywire was gruff.

"Yeah, I get tired of you moaning about how much you like it, and why don't they get it."

Darlene ignored this, and took the box from him, placing it on the counter.

"Thank you!" She shyly kissed his cheek. He blushed and pretended to fight her off. The boys giggled. The atmosphere was lighter that night. They all joined in a card game, and the boys shrieked and giggled each time one of them "won" a round. The fire was warm, the tea was hot, and there was peace in the air.

It was all fine for a week or so. Krie and Haywire and Darlene watched CBC North.

"Gimme $20," Darlene said to the TV.

"Darlene, we have everything we need. Why do you need $20?"

"Going to the store tomorrow. Gonna make the boys something special as a coming home surprise. Come on!" Haywire awkwardly fished a bill out of his tight jeans.

"Makin' more tea." Darlene didn't come back from the kitchen. After 15 minutes, Haywire got up and checked on her.

"She's gone."

"Where? I didn't hear the door."

"She was trying to be quiet. Going for beer, I guess. Old John down the way is a bootlegger."

It was an hour or so before they heard someone loudly singing. One of the boys looked up.

"Oh, oh. Mom had happy juice!"

They all looked up when the door banged open. Darlene staggered in, smiling, hair messy, with an open case of beer dangling from one arm.

She sang.

"Why don't you love me like you used to do." She answered her own question, yelling the last two words. "Because I'm not Leah, that's why, and because you NEVER DID!"

The boys started. The eldest didn't move from his spot on the rug but shrugged his shoulders as if he expected a blow. The youngest bolted under the coffee table.

"Darlene, settle the hell down."

"Why, so we can pretend everything's fine?" She was mocking.

"Dammit, Darlene, don't you care about these boys?"

"Do you?"

"You know I do. Go sleep it off!" Haywire was plying Ronnie out from under the table. He had attached his arms and legs to Haywire's arm like a little sloth. He was pale and his eyes wide. Haywire cuddled him.

"Darlene, go!"

"Can't stand the sight of me?" she challenged, swaying.

"Darlene, I'm warning you."

"What are you gonna do, make me?"

The air was ugly with emotion. Krie winced.

"Darlene, stop."

"*Darr-leene*, stop." Her voice was sarcastic, jeering.

Haywire lit a smoke, threw the match in the ashtray with a little too much force.

Krie was soaring above the river, enjoying a turn on the breeze. On the shore Tina was waving him down. He swooped, circled, and landed in front of her. He was excited by her tight jeans; her top that revealed her breasts. He stepped closer, allowed her hands to roam his body. He moaned. She kissed him behind his ear, he shivered, waves of pleasure raising his skin. He kissed him across the neck, and then her lips were on his. Hot, sweet, her tongue teasing its way between his open lips. He moaned again, his breath coming in pants. She crouched slowly as she lifted his shirt, kissed and licked down from his chest to his waist.

"DARLENE, get the fuck out of here!" Krie snapped awake, at the sound of Haywire's voice, a tone he had never heard. Darlene was crouched over Krie, with a triumphant leer, looking toward Haywire in the doorway.

"Jealous?" she slurred.

Crying reached them from the boys' room. Haywire gently called, "It's alright Billy, we're playing a game. I'll be in there in a minute." Through tight lips, with a dangerous quiet to his voice, Haywire spoke slowly.

"Darlene, get out of this house. NOW. And the boys stay here. Don't set foot back here. Ever." Krie was frozen, felt ill. His erection felt like a log. Too late, covered it with his pillow. He sat up. He was hot with shame.

"Haywire, I didn't …"

"Not now, Krie." Haywire's tone was harsh. Krie felt tears of despair well into his eyes. Darlene said nothing. She lurched past Haywire with the same sick smile and left the house. Krie was flooded with emotion. How could he not have known it was Darlene? How could he have responded to her? What was he going to say to Haywire? What if this ruined everything? There was evil cackling from the closet.

"Get out!" Krie hissed.

"Don't worry, I'm going." The Bonewalker's voice chilled him to his marrow.

He did not sleep for the rest of the night. Distracted, both he and Haywire had not remembered to put protection medicine around the house.

It had been a pretty lousy day, but Krie brightened when he heard Uncle Angus's voice in the house from the front door. He kicked the fresh snow off his boots and ran for Uncle. He hugged him tight, and Uncle laughed. He could feel his happiness.

"You, okay?" He looked at Krie, brows furrowed, serious.

"Yeah, Uncle, it's great to see you!"

"You, too. Ran outta tea," Krie knew this was an excuse.

"You didn't medicine this house."

"I know, and he got in through Darlene."

"That's why I'm here. We take care of it. Now."

When Krie came out, they were placing bits of something at each door and window. Uncle was serious.

"Gramma said to change this often. That Bonewalker is waiting for any chance he can get. We won't give it to him."

Haywire nodded. He looked miserable. It was then that Krie realized he hadn't slept all night either.

It was better for the boys. They kept the house happy, and Uncle played with them for the week that he stayed. They counted with him in the language,

"*Ethega, (ethega) hleketeta (hleketeta), tadida, (tadida) hlen'ta (hlen'ta).*"

Krie guessed words with them. The boys yelled the words in glee back at Uncle.

"*Tli* (Dog)! *Keda* (Moose)! *Sas* (Bear)! *Gah* (Rabbit)!"

Krie would end up rolling on the floor laughing, the boys moiling like spawning salmon, rolling all over him. Uncle would put on a grumpy face and mock being an offended teacher. This only made them laugh harder. Haywire would sit shaking his head, a big smile on his face. The tension had gone in Darlene's wake, but behind the trees in the outside dark, the Bonewalker had not.

Uncle and Haywire had the truck loaded to go. Krie's heart flew.

"Krie, pack your stuff, we're heading back to the cabin." Krie's heart was light as he stuffed his clothes into his duffle. He did not realize until this moment how much being out there at Little Annie meant to him; how connected to the land he felt, and how much he looked forward to running the traps. It was more; it was about being with Angus and Haywire and being where they had always been.

The headlights pierced the winter black, and the tires squeaked loudly in the snow on the way out to the road. The boys played in the back quietly, and the men were silent. Krie's spirit swam in the warm waters of these silences. When they arrived, they all smelled the smoke from the stove. They glanced at one another. There was no sign of a vehicle, a snow-mobile. Then they heard a dog bark. They smiled at one another. Krie's curiosity was high. Someone was in the cabin, and that someone had brought a dog.

When they were closer, they smelled delicious aromas of cooking. Whoever it was, Krie thought, they knew their way around a kitchen! He noticed the woodpile was high with freshly cut wood, and he knew that the water pails inside would be full. Whoever was in the cabin had been here a day or two.

"Lorna!" Krie was happy to see his cousin. She had the table filled with bannock, plates and bowls, and there was something bubbling in the large pot. She even had the tea ready.

"Thought you guys'd be hungry by now." Nobody questioned, but after all the gear was hauled in, everyone sat at the table. Lorna said in a gentle tone, "You young pups can sit on the floor to eat." They seemed happy enough with this and played while they waited. It was funny about kids, Krie thought, how pliant they were with whatever went on. He wished he were.

"Got a message from Gramma Maisey." The men looked up at her.

"Says you need to bring Krie there tomorrow."

"Okay," said Uncle. It seemed to Krie that Angus took this as a soldier would take orders. Unquestioning.

"We run traps first thing," Uncle said. Krie wished he could sleep in; it WAS Saturday, but part of him was excited to see what might be waiting for them. And what did Gramma Maisey want with him?

It was dusk when they got to Gramma Maisey's. Krie's body ached all over from the hike through buckbrush and uneven frozen muskeg. How did Haywire and Angus do this at their ages? he wondered. Through the short jack pines was the glow of the cabin windows. Maisey's little bear dog did not bark as they neared up to the cabin but wagged it's whole behind in welcome. Krie smelled the aroma of dinner before they opened the door, and his stomach growled. Living in the bush, he was growing accustomed to long hours without food, but this was a hot dinner he was going to appreciate! Gramma welcomed them all, "Tea, bannock *deh*."

Krie loved her accent. They poured scalding tea and devoured bannock before Gramma Maisey brought steaming plates of meat, potatoes and carrots. Krie's eyes were watering with hunger. Maisey motioned to Krie and said, "Make a spirit plate." He did so, carefully, and waited.

"Take it to the tree down the hill, you'll know where." He went out the door, and the bear dog followed him. He saw the tree and knew, just as Gramma had said. He said his prayer and left the offering in a perfect spot the branches provided. The little dog wagged its tail, and Krie bent to pet her.

"I'll bring you a treat after, okay, Lady?"

He swore the dog's tail wagged harder. He knew this dog was always spoken to in Tagish. The dog knew before he turned to walk back to the cabin. It was then Krie caught that the dog was in on this non-verbal thing. In the flow, in the moment, able to know what was coming next.

Gramma's laugh reminded Krie of trees creaking in the breeze. His spirits rose, and the energy from the moose meat surged through him.

"Moose nose," her eyes flashed.

"May I please have more?"

Gramma smiled and nodded toward the stove.

After bannock and jam, with their teacups filled, Krie could see the men relax, their muscles letting go in their chairs.

"Anything?" Gramma asked Haywire.

"Nope. Something is stealing from the traps."

"What?"

"Coyote tracks. Lots. Lots."

"Hee, hee, hee. Her laugh was like a squeaky cabin door.

"Yeah, I'll put something out for him next time."

"Good, Grand-sonny." She did not look in his direction, but Krie knew she was speaking to him when she said, "*Nda.*"

He followed silently to her back room. It was sparse, with a bed, neatly made, and a tiny table beside it with an old-fashioned oil lamp. There was one old photograph on the wall, and a dresser. She motioned him to stay standing in the middle of the room. He closed his eyes. He heard a dresser drawer open. He felt gentle hands on him and submitted wholly. Gramma's voice was quiet in the language and enveloped him like a blanket. She moved around him, and he felt her hands, smelled a medicine. She spoke gently, as she continued her work. Through his eyelids, he saw the light become bright in the room, as though an electric light had been turned on. He squeezed his eyes closed tighter.

"*Shadeniht'eh*," she whispered, with love in her voice. He began to cry, silent tears raining down his cheeks. He knew she could see all that had happened to him. He felt like he wanted to throw up.

"It's okay," she said, and he vomited. She carefully wiped him up, and he heard her cross the room, and come back. The smell of his vomit was terrible.

"Good," she said, her voice caressing his sad heart.

A heat rose from his feet to his head, and he staggered, as dizziness overcame him. He sank to his knees and fought the waves that threatened to take him. He felt her hands on his head, stroking gently from his crown down his hair and shoulders. The light was brighter. He began to vibrate, his whole body shaking at lightning speed. He allowed this and relaxed into it.

"That's good," she said.

The light behind his eyes was brighter still. The vibration was almost moving his body across the floor. The hands moved the air around him. He felt as if he were floating. He felt as though he wanted to fly. There was a deep peace that rooted him to the earth. A peace he almost did not remember. She spoke in the language, the words caressing his troubled spirit. His whole being felt a calm descend like a waterfall, over his head, his shoulders, and running down his entire body. There was pulsing vibration. Her voice was a gentle sigh, a caress, with the sweetness that he had heard others talk to infants. There was one lightning-like flash of even brighter light, and then, it was still, he was still, and he could hear the soft hiss of the oil lamp. She stood back, and he could hear her pray still. He smelled sweet medicine. He inhaled the sense of peace, of calm. He felt at this moment as if nothing could ever harm him. As though he could face anything and conquer. He felt rooted to earth, and yet, sensed that he was connected even to the stars outside in the sky. The vibration was very subtle; more like an awareness of energy. He felt everything and was part of it all. It was like swimming in a warm lake. He allowed this to be, allowed himself to be within it all.

"Good," her voice was full of encouragement, and satisfaction. "Take some time, now."

He stood quietly, for he did not know for how long, as she stood with him. When he opened his eyes, Uncle and Haywire were standing in the room. Krie reached his arms out for Gramma Maisey and held her tenderly. Tears ran down his cheeks and he whispered in her ear: "*Meegwitch, Gunalcheeshe.*" When she pulled out of his arms, he saw she had tears of her own.

"Sonny, you're a good boy. You be alright."

☉☉◎

Monday, the school bus dropped Krie with other kids from outside Carcross. Albert Ross noticed the bundle around Krie's neck. He reached for it, and Krie caught his hand, knowing it should not be touched. Albert was a little slow, so Krie spoke kindly.

"No, Albert, don't touch it, okay?" Albert's face fell a little.

"Hey, Albert, let's play a game of checkers later, okay?"

Albert loved checkers. His face rose into a grin. Just then Ben Abraham strolled up. He wore his pants too tight, and had the face of a hunting, hungry coyote with dangerously angry eyes.

"Hey you creepy Cree, stop eyeing up my girlfriend, or I will pound your ass." Albert's grin disappeared.

"Ben, Tiffanie is my lab partner. I'm not interested in her. You have nothing to worry about."

"Are you saying she's a dog?"

"Don't be an ass, I just mean I know she's your girlfriend, and I'm not after her."

"You better not be, 'Pervy Post.'"

Krie's blood turned to ice, and a fire rose within. His voice was dangerously quiet.

"WHAT did you call me?"

"I know who your Dad is. You look just like him."

"Whether you do, or whether you don't, it's none of your damned business."

"Yeah, what are you gonna do about it?"

"I'm gonna kick your stupid ass." Krie was right in his face. He could smell the fear but knew that the crowd that had silently materialized around them made it impossible for Ben to lose face. He also knew that Ben knew how to fight. He had a rock in his stomach, knowing this was going to hurt.

"At lunch, around back."

"I'll be there," Krie spat the words in his face.

He had few friends here, because he did not care to make them. They formed a circle in the playing field and they waited, as if for a starter gun. There he was, sauntering out of the bush with his girlfriend wrapped around him like a winter scarf. A smoke dangled from sneering lips, and he sauntered over with a swagger, pushing his way into the circle. His girlfriend kissed him.

"Pound his ass!" The thrill in her voice like glass.

Ben slowly circled Krie. Krie kept his eyes on him, began moving to ensure he was facing him. A lightening thought came to Krie. Rather, he heard Uncle's voice.

"Bear dog."

Krie understood, he must be quick like lightning striking with no warning, and he must aggravate the bear to chase it from the camp by being untouchable. He recalled watching Ben in other fights. He was by no means fast, but he knew how to hit, and hard. Krie glided on his toes, weightless. The crowd voices got louder, more excited, but Krie heard nothing. He dodged the first three punches, and only Ben heard the voices get higher with excitement. "This is gonna be a gooder."

"Maybe this isn't gonna be a straight KO!"

"Yeah, Ben'll get 'im, just wait."

"This guy ain't scared though" That comment struck Ben's gut hard. He was unnerved. If Krie wasn't afraid, what did he have to use as his weapon?

Ben hit home, a good right, and Krie breathed in, jerking back at the last second when he knew he was unable to entirely dodge the blow. He acted as if it didn't even touch him, took a deep breath, and danced harder and faster, back, forth, back forth, circling with Ben. Ben's face was red, and he looked uglier than usual.

"Filthy Cree, you think you're so shit-hot."

"I am who I am," Krie replied, his voice even.

"Well, I'm gonna make you wish you weren't."

"There isn't a person on this planet that can do that."

Ben's face reddened further, and he spat in Krie's direction. Krie dodged, and the spit from Ben hit Ben's best friend, Ralph.

"Gross; asshole!"

Ben gritted his teeth and stuck out his jaw. Out came his chest. Krie knew what he was going to do; he telegraphed it in his eyes. He dodged the upper cut and struck lightning fast with a right upper cut and a liver shot. Ben staggered hard and his face went white. Ben heard crowd roar, and that the tide changed. Fear gripped his innards. This had never happened.

"Krie, nail his ass!"

"Yeah, show him the little bitch he is." One feeble female voice.

"Come on, Ben, be careful!" One loyal voice.

There was a fire in Ben's eyes. Krie's blood was cool as ice. He danced harder, faster, circles around Ben. He started laughing, a low bitter laugh. Then he saw the fear. This was the moment. He planted himself, breathed deep, hands up beside his face, he struck hard and fast and with no warning, even in his eyes.

Krie landed a right jab, ducked and glided to the left as Ben threw a looping hard right. Anticipating a big left, Krie landed a quick left to the body and stepped out of the way as the punch swung past his face. He immediately stepped back into range and landed a hard-left cross to Ben's jaw. Krie watched as Ben's eyes rolled back, and he slowly fell like a downed tree. Left, right, chest, gut. He'd remember that combo. Ben was on the ground, still, white, and he was out cold.

"KO!" he heard someone yell.

Ben's girlfriend turned on her heel, disgust on her face, and walked back to the school. The crowd chanted.

"KO, KO, KO" over and over. Krie stood, feeling the sweat pouring all over him, burning into his eyes. He felt every cell of his body. He felt his breath tearing in and out his lungs, hot and dry. He felt hands pounding his back. Big Albert was lifting him right off the ground and swinging him with a raptured look on his face.

"You showed the bully, Krie, didn't you?"

"Guess I did, Albert."

That night Gramma Maisey called Krie into her room. She was on the bed; a single candle creating a warm glow.

"Sonny don't fight. Walk away. You may be young and full of piss and vinegar, but remember you have strong power. I know. I am old. Should be gone now, long time. I live between. One Moccasin here, one there, in that next world. Angus say Bonewalker is smoke and mirrors. Doctoring, that is smoke and mirrors too. Healers, we use that person's own power. Talk to their spirit. Work with it. Now you work with your spirit. Same way. Use that courage. Love. Look for it. The only fight is with Bonewalker. You fight hard, use your power. We all gonna help you. But don't fight people. Take up your power. Don't think about anything else. Just making your power stronger. Just do that."

Krie nodded. He felt a glow in his belly, and he reached over and kissed Gramma Maisey. She grinned, she nodded.

Krie had just woken up when he noticed his nose wasn't dog cold. He listened, and heard the drip, drip, drip of water off the cabin roof. Curious, he rose and looked out. The sun warmed the land, and he could see the snow had changed. Within a few weeks, the snow was receding off the lake. Walking up to meet the school bus, he felt the sun on his back, warmer each day, and it felt good to leave the heavy winter coat at home. He watched as the land burst to life, the changes overnight, and the air was full of the fresh smell of a thousand kinds of green and sun warmed earth.

His heart sang like the birds outside the window.

"Grandmother Sopiah!"

"Yes," she said, joy and laughter in her voice.

"I'm coming up for the summer, Krie."

He could hardly wait to tell Haywire and Angus.

Krie thought his impatience was what made the months crawl by. The most eventful thing was gaffing in the creek for fish. The creek was a five-minute walk away from the lake and up the trail from the cabin. Uncle went ahead, Haywire had the gaff hook. Haywire straddled the little creek, and dropped the gaff hook in hard. When he pulled it back up, several fish were on the prongs. He carefully removed them with gloved hands, and they flopped on the bank. Krie put them in the bucket. Haywire plunged the gaff until the bucket was full. Krie returned to the cabin and brought more buckets.

"Good run," Angus noted. They fried fish for dinner, boiled some in soup and dried the rest over a smoky fire. It was kept in a paper bag on the table for snacks.

The days passed until school end, and Krie was not sorry to hear the doors close behind him at the end of June. He was excited, thinking about Grandmother Sopiah's arrival, when he heard a cackle behind him. The hair rose on the back of his neck. He did not turn, but muttered,

"You don't scare me, Bonewalker."

"Fear. You have fear, and I know how to pull it out of you." Krie flipped his backpack onto his shoulder and walked toward the bus. As the bus pulled away, he saw Dale Post leering at him from where he leaned on the flagpole. He pulled a face as the Bonewalker waved and put his head back to laugh. Krie was glad he couldn't hear it from where he sat. It was bad enough that he could see Bonewalker through the window. He looked forward but could not shake a feeling of creeping dread.

Finally, it was the first of July, and they were off to the White-horse airport. On either side of the gravel road between Little Annie and the main road to town, the land rose to mountains. Dormant, winter-covered land was newly alive with a hundred shades of green trees rolling up the mountainsides. You could feel the heat and it was only 7 a.m.

"Gonna be a hot one," Haywire said, as he lit a smoke.

Krie laughed as a porcupine wove awkwardly in front of the truck, and Haywire slowed so it made its way off to the side.

"Too bad we are in a hurry. That would have made a good welcome dinner for Grandmother," Krie grinned.

"Show respect, Krie."

"Sorry." Haywire smiled at him. Krie admonished himself within for not greeting the animal as they passed. This, he knew, would ensure they would always have enough to eat. It was disrespectful to speak about a live animal as food. Even if it was. There was so much to learn. To remember.

"Krie, I know you understand." He smiled at Haywire knowing his thoughts.

Standing in the airport crowd, Krie craned his neck to see Grandmother Sopiah. She was the last one in, and he was taken aback when he saw how thin she was, and how she walked slowly on the arm of a woman in uniform. As Grand-mother's eyes found Krie, her face relaxed into a broad peaceful smile. Krie flew to her and embraced her tightly. He began to cry, silently, his chest and shoulders shaking.

"My boy, my precious boy," Grandmother cooed so only he could hear. After a time, she said, "Let me look at you." Holding his shoulders at arm's length, she gazed deeply at him, as though her eyes were drinking him.

"What a handsome boy, Krie, more so than I imagined, and look how TALL you are. All that wild meat really agrees with you." He embraced her again and lifted her off the floor as she laughed in mock protest. He spun her. She protested but did not stop laughing when he set her gently on her feet. Haywire embraced her, and she was still laughing when she said, "Well, thank goodness you are a little more reserved; I'm not sure I would survive another spin."

During the drive to Little Annie, all the way to the Charlie cabin, Grandmother held Krie's hand in hers as he pointed out green high up on the mountainsides.

"I love the fresh of the air; never mind the dust, it's so clean up here; it's as if you can catch the layers of fragrance." She smiled as Krie spoke about the winter trapping, the spring gaffing of fish, and school. Near the junction, Grandmother asked Haywire. "Would you mind if we made a stop at Maisey's?"

"Be a good idea; she will have bannock and dinner ready."

He was right. As they walked up the little path to her cabin, the aromas of fresh bannock and wild meat reached them. Gramma Maisey was waiting at the door, and Angus was inside at the table, smiling to beat all. Maisey embraced Sopiah tenderly and kissed her on both cheeks.

"It's been far too long. How long will you stay?"

"As long as it takes."

"Good, come in. Tea, bannock and meat there."

Later, Krie and Grandmother were walking along the creek.

"Grandmother, did you know Gramma Maisey from before?"

"Yes, my boy, we have been friends for many years."

"What about Uncle Angus?"

Grandmother wore an expression of sadness, and as if she was seeing something far off in the distance.

"I loved Uncle Angus, Krie, and I still do. Just because a person is no longer with us does not mean there is not still love." Grandmother and Uncle Angus? Krie was stunned.

Then he understood her words. Krie felt ice all over creeping from his toes to his head. His face was white.

"Uncle Angus … is dead?"

Krie's mind was moving all over like the creek at gaffing time, filled with seeming impossibilities. Why did he see the dead? And why could he not tell the difference between them and the living? And why had Haywire not said anything? He obviously could see him, too! Krie felt ill, like he wanted to throw up and move his bowels at the same time. He was quiet for days, until there was a time that he was alone in the cabin with the two Grandmothers. He knew they had sent Haywire on a trip that he didn't need to make to the store in Tagish. He came in from where he was walking by the creek, trying to clear his thoughts.

"Grammas?"

"Yes, my boy?"

"Why can I see the dead?"

"Because you are very gifted."

"Why can't I tell the difference between the dead and the living?"

"You will learn." Gramma Maisey's voice was soothing.

"How will I?"

"Have you ever seen tiny points of light that flash around Uncle?"

"Yes, when I first met him."

"There you are, my boy. Those are other spirits. They don't need you to see them."

"So, spirits decide who is going to see them?"

"When you see them all the time, like Uncle, yes."

"I saw how Uncle looked at you when you came in, Grandmother. He loves you very much, and not just love."

Grandmother blushed and looked very shy. She held silence as they walked.

"Long ago, we spoke of marriage. We were very young."

"Oh," Krie was touched.

"I had big plans, I came here to meet our relatives, the descendants of a woman who came North and stayed long ago. She helped your Mother to fight the Bonewalker."

"I want to hear more about her."

"In time. I came, and Angus and I fell for each other, but we found we were related, very distant relations and the same clans. I was Raven; he is Raven. Here it is forbidden for relatives, even distant, to marry. I am Raven because my ancestor from here was. You already know clans are passed through the women, that and names." Krie nodded.

"It was heartbreaking for us, but we moved on in our lives. We never forgot each other. I don't know about him, but I never stopped loving him."

"Do you think that is why he is around?" Krie looked searchingly at Grandmother.

"I am sure that is part of it, and I think you should ask him."

"I will." Krie's jaw was set. "I will."

Later, after Krie and Haywire went to bed, the Grandmothers stayed up very late talking by candlelight and sipping tea. Krie listened, half asleep.

"You know, Sopiah, it has been generations that the same Bonewalker has been trying to take our family members."

"No!"

"Yes! Started with Lightning Medicine Woman. Got ill. Almost died because of it. Someone from her homeland. Jealous. Called up the thing."

"How do people with gifts do such terrible things?"

"I just don't know. With power to heal and help others, yet they use it to harm."

"I will never understand, never!"

"Sad thing. Those people need prayers more than others."

As the days went by, Krie saw that Grandmother Sopiah was not as quick as she used to be. It took time for her to get up from a chair to walk to the truck. It wasn't just that. She was much thinner than before. She got tired easily. Sometimes she would go very pale and tremble slightly, closing her eyes. He finally asked her.

"Grandmother, I have noticed you seem to be suffering from some pain, and you have changed."

"My boy, I am very sick, and I will die sooner than I would have." Tears edged their way down his cheeks and his heart hurt so hard in his chest that it seemed it would burst.

"Why, Grandmother, and can't Gramma Maisey just heal you?"

"There are things that can't be healed once they are past a point."

"When did you find out you were sick?"

"After your Auntie passed. I never got my energy back, so I went to the doctor. The tests showed abnormalities in my blood. I got a diagnosis just now. It was already too late for healing."

"How long, Grandmother?" The pain had taken over so that he could barely breathe, let alone speak.

"It's difficult to say, Krie, but I don't think long at all." She held him in her arms as he cried.

"I will stay here, Krie, until the time comes, alright?" He was unable to speak, the pain had enveloped his being, blinding him like a fog. He nodded, and she held him as night fell silently.

Before dawn, Krie was up and ready. He saw Angus already by the creek. They smiled at one another as they walked along the creek in silence. After a time, Angus stopped, turned, and looked at Krie.

"You can fight the Bonewalker. Anyone can fight it and win. Just believe you can. Bonewalker finds your fear, your weakness. It attacks it. You are fighting your fear. Fear feels very powerful. It is not. Your belief – your strength – is more powerful. Your spirit is forever. You are you, and there is only one you; that is your power.

"I have the gift of teachings, of belief which help a person find the gifts within themselves, those weapons of spiritual battle. Those teachings create a light that is so bright that it can blind those who would attack. Bonewalkers are hard to blind, but it can be done." Angus stood quiet as Grandmother Sopiah approached.

"Shall we sing up the sun, my boy?" She did not see Angus who stood with them, smiling at Krie as bright as the rising sun.

"Uncle was talking to me about beating the Bonewalker, Grandmother, but I am so sensitive; everything around me causes pain because I can feel everybody. I feel the pain in my chest or my gut. Some people make me dizzy. I've learned to ignore it or focus or be in the now for hunting. I'm looking for something but don't know what. Like I'm searching for lost treasure but in myself."

"My boy, you are searching for the same thing we all are. You are searching for what is inside of you."

"That's what Uncle was trying to tell me. I don't feel safe with anyone but you, Uncle, Gramma Maisey, and Haywire. I'm looking for my safe people, knowing that they can't help me."

"The safe person you are looking for is you." They stood silently for a time. She sighed.

"Uncertainty is actually a place of great power. In that moment, anything is possible. Focus on one or two potentials; it makes those things more of a possibility. Think only positive thoughts because our thoughts are wood for the fire of our creative energy."

Krie was silent as they stood, listening to the creek sing in the silence.

◉◉◉

Grief in preparation for someone leaving the earth is a strange thing. It brings the weakness out in people. Stupidity reigns. Bad behaviours and stupid arguments are the norms.

Krie chose to stay to himself. He felt his vulnerability. He recognized it when looking for lost socks brought tears to his eyes. He withdrew and only spoke when it would be rude not to. It did not go unnoticed. He was left to himself as he knew the others were wise enough to recognize it. They all stayed at Gramma Maisey's. There was no real privacy in a three-room cabin, but all were comforted by the presence of the others. There was an easy silence between them, and though Gramma Maisey and Grandmother Sopiah were concerned for Krie, they left him to his thoughts.

"Split wood," Uncle advised.

"You can let out a lot of mean when you split wood."

Krie split a lot of wood in the coming days.

"Goodness, my boy, we got enough for two winters," Gramma Maisey giggled in her scratchy old voice."

Krie was out exerting his muscles at the wood stump. Just when the axe was about to drop, he heard a shout.

"Your leg!" He wavered, and to his horror, the axe fell, embedding itself in his lower right leg. The Bonewalker ran off through the woods, cackling, triumphant, hurling insults all the way.

Krie called for Haywire. Something in the tone of his voice made Haywire run from the door. Krie stood holding the axe where it was, knowing the bleeding would be worse when it was removed. Haywire's voice was serious.

"Krie, hold it right there, I'll be back."

The Grandmothers were efficient and calm. They had cloths and water. Maisey went off to collect pitch from a nearby tree.

Haywire cut Krie's jeans up to his knee and rolled them out of the way.

"Krie, you would have needed stitches, but Gramma Maisey knows what she is doing, okay?"

Krie nodded. The sight of his own blood was making him nauseous. Dizziness made his head buzz, and his eyes saw darkness like a cloud of flies in front of him. He fought it by deep breathing.

"That's good," Grandmother Sopiah's voice was soft. "Keep that up."

She had tied a cloth tight above the wound, and the blood was slowing. Maisey brought out a bowl. Krie looked at his blood in the snow, and on the axe that lay on the ground.

"Who died, by an axe?"

His voice was quiet. Everyone froze.

"A man, a man was felled with an axe, the woman, my Mother! What happened to her?"

"Your Mother killed your Father. It was an accident. It was a terrible thing. It was what made her mind sick." Gramma Maisey's voice sounded as though she was soothing a sick baby.

Tears poured down Krie's face. He said nothing while the wound was cleaned with black spruce water and the gap closed with melted pitch. His leg was well-bandaged with cotton cloth.

"What happened?" Gramma Maisey was serious.

"Bonewalker," was all Krie said.

"I thought so." Maisey was angry.

"I'm sorry, Gramma Maisey. I know I should have been focusing."

"You have to – it's life and death out here," said Angus.

"I'm sorry." Krie's voice was miserable. "It won't happen again."

"Bonewalker knew you were vulnerable." Grandmother's voice was sad.

"I should have warned you, my boy."

"No, Grandmother, I should have known. Now I do."

"I should have told you to use courage born from love when you are more open to attack."

The pitch on his wound tightened as it hardened, and the throbbing was soothed by it.

"Sorry, Haywire, I won't be much help to you for a couple of days."

"Krie, things happen, accidents happen."

"I have had firsthand experience with a Bonewalker," Grandmother Sopiah broke the silence by the river.

"You did?"

"My Father. We called him 'Crazy Eyes', our code name when we knew he wasn't him."

"What do you mean 'he wasn't him?'"

"His eyes were wild and terrified when the Bonewalker was in him, and there was crazy fire in the front, and his fear in behind, like he was cowering behind Bonewalker."

"Grandmother, how did you beat him?"

"My Father killed himself, my boy, and Bonewalker found another host."

"Host?"

"They need a host to walk around in. They search for someone vulnerable and weak, someone who is addicted."

"Oh, kind of like vampires or werewolves or something?"

"Sort of, and eventually they go crazy because they don't understand it wasn't, them who did whatever awful things they recall."

"So, Dale Post was not responsible?"

"He let himself be taken over. He did not fight or did not fight hard enough. He did not seek help.'\"

"Maybe I should pray for my Father."

"I believe, my boy, you should call on him for help."

"This is confusing; I hate him for what he did, but he can help me?"

"I think it will help him in the next world, my boy, if you call on him to fight."

"I've hated him for so long."

"I know, Krie, it's hard not to hate someone who did what he did, but it really was not him."

"I hate him for his weakness."

"We should never hate anyone for anything."

"It's hard, Grandmother."

"Yes, my boy." Her gentle hand was on his shoulder.

"Krie remember my Father did the same to me as Dale Post did to you." Krie's head turned to face her. Tears were on her face. He took her hands in his. He did not want to hear more, but he knew he had to for his sake and for Grandmother's.

"I have told you how my Father drugged me. I have told you about his Bonewalker. But it is not the only one I had to fight. There was a time when I was young. I moved to Whitehorse. I wanted to be independent. I got a job and a place to live, and then something happened.

"I was walking home from work one night. There were no buses back then. It was not well-lit in that area. A car with two men stopped. They offered me a ride. Offered beer. When I refused, they pointed a gun at me, and I was forced into the car. They held me for days in a house of horror on Lake Laberge. There were more men there. It was a gang clubhouse. I was used by everyone who walked in. They kept me in a dog cage, and I was only allowed out when someone wanted to use me. I would not call it sex. It was a terrible act of violation each time. I did not know humans could do things like that to other humans. If I did not scream, I was hit and punched until I cried out. I learned to do it as soon as they unlocked the cage. Fear aroused them. The only thing that kept me alive was the thought of escape. But it was impossible. I was locked in. I never had enough food or water, so I was weak.

"One night, an Indian man unlocked me. He motioned me to silence. Something in his demeanour made me comply. He gave me water. Covered me with a blanket. He spoke the language. I understood, even though it was nothing like Saulteaux. I knew he was telling me to stay quiet and to follow him and, no matter what happened, to run for my life. My heart was pounding so hard it thundered in my ears. I was terrified. We crept between passed-out bodies, and we got away. I saw the dogs I had heard over the weeks. They were lying on the ground, I guessed he had knocked them out somehow. We got down to the lake. He motioned for me to get in and swim. We swam a long way in the dark."

I said to him, "I have to go to the police, tell them what's going on in there."

"No," he said. "If you speak of this, those men will hunt you down and kill you."

"I never knew how that man knew I was there, or why he risked his life to get me out. He had long hair in a braid, and Sundance scars I saw in the moonlight. A lot of them. Chest, arms, back. We swam for what seemed hours, and when I got too tired, he got me to put my arms around his neck and lay over top of him while he swam. That brother saved my life. He had a truck way on the far side of the lake. We got to his truck, and he had clothes, food, and water. He made me eat slow. We drove a long way that night. We got to a cabin by another lake. I felt safe, and in that cabin was a wonderful, and loving woman. She said nothing, but sat me down and gave me fish soup. It was the most delicious soup I ever had to this day. I tasted her love in that soup. She nursed me for days, sang to me, and prayed over me. She was wonderful. The man would bring us wild meat. I stayed for a long time, maybe two months. She talked to me about Bonewalkers. It was then I finally understood my Father."

There was a cold snap. It went down to 60 below. The Grandmothers made Krie moose hide mitts and mukluks with fur trim. His feet in the snow made a sound like a squeaky old floor on steroids. He kind of liked it. The air tickled his nose with frost that formed around his sparse moustache hairs. It hurt to talk, made him cough. A cover on his mouth helped, but only just.

Haywire taught Krie to snowshoe. How to breathe in the cold, so his lungs would not be harmed by the frigid air. Breathe in through the nose, hold, blow out through the mouth. Snowshoeing was much more strenuous than Krie had imagined. As they crossed the lake together, clouds of steam rose above them. They stopped at the cabin on the way back and made tea.

"Okay, now you know how to run traps without a Ski-Doo, you think you can do it on snowshoes now?" Krie nodded.

Grandmother Sopiah's voice was soft, "My rescuer's old Grandmother was so kind to me. That young man fell in love with me. I could not stay with him, because I felt I was garbage, that he deserved much, much better. I wanted to love him, he was so good, so kind. I loved him, but I did not think that I could love him the way he deserved after what he had done for me. He said he saw power in me. Great power. I did not see it. We learned we were related through a relative who came North a couple of generations before and married a man from Carcross. We couldn't be together even if I wanted. By that time, I loved him with all that I was.

"I left and went back to Winnipeg. I met this tall, gorgeous Saulteaux. He was full of jokes and stories and had a way of making me feel like I was the only woman in the world. *That's* a joke. He took me out, and we had so much fun. We danced all night. He acted like a gentleman. I say acted because he turned out to be anything but!

"I knew nothing about drugs. He used them with needles. I only found them when he left. He would come home raging and accuse me of sleeping with other men. He would wake me up and claim he saw a man leaving the apartment and beat me. I recognized the Bonewalker in him, but I was far too weak and terrified to deal with it this time. I loved him. I could not leave him. I kept seeing hope until he went too far. I saw in his eyes this was true. This man's Uncle had been a powerful medicine man. This man who was already in the next world came to me in dreams and helped me. Told me over and over he was going to give me a chance to get out of this, and to watch for that chance and to take it. This good man was like my good Father.

"The bad man would not remember the next day what he had done. One night, he beat me so badly my face was black and blue. He came in the morning laughing and joking and then wondered why I wasn't answering him. I simply said maybe he should come closer and have a look. He did. The sorrow in his face was terrible. He went to the window. Stood there looking out for the longest time. And then he asked if I wanted him to leave. I hesitated. I remembered what Uncle had said. I just said, 'Yes.' He left, and I never saw him again. And then I missed him like I had lost an arm."

◉◉◎

Trapping on snowshoes was no joke. It was a hard go. Krie guessed the rough, uneven terrain was a better workout than those late-night extreme fighting workouts advertised on TV. He was covered in sweat, everywhere but his face. It was still deep cold. Haywire had warned him no matter how hot he got to not remove his jacket and if his body got too cold, to tell him right away. The problem was this kind of cold was different. It numbed you before you realized what the danger was. He figured if he kept moving, the blood would flow. He couldn't really feel his legs.

They had all small animals in the traps. By the time they reached Gramma Maisey's Krie was having difficulty getting his legs to do what he wanted. He willed them to move.

"I need the outhouse."

Haywire nodded, heading toward the cache to stow the animals. Krie got out of sight and got his pants down. He grabbed mittfuls of snow and rubbed his legs with it, hard, fast, and thoroughly. He put them back on and did a slow walk to the cabin. He knew enough to go to the other room where it was colder. There he stayed until he felt his circulation come back. He wished he didn't. The pain of the veins and vessels warming was excruciating. Gramma Maisey came in.

"Chilblains, sonny?" He nodded, miserably. She rubbed his legs, and the pain increased.

"Let's warm you." She massaged him, and he gritted his teeth. He heard the cackle outside the window. Maisey ignored it.

"We gonna get you long-johns tomorrow."

"Yeah, I think I need them!"

"You got to watch now your legs know how to freeze. Like that Bonewalker, when he knows how to get in."

Krie felt foolish but swore to himself that this would never happen again.

Sunday, Krie was hauling water when Grandmother Sopiah came down to the creek where he had re-chopped the water hole in the ice. He felt her before he saw her. She was smiling. He put down the bucket and embraced her, hard.

"My boy," she crooned in his ear.

"Grandmother, I am going to finish that Bonewalker, for us all."

"You will do more than that, Krie. You will fight other Bonewalkers for others, too, throughout your life. You are a Warrior." He looked deep into her eyes. He was drinking her in. She saw his jaw tighten, and he straightened.

"Yes, Grandmother, I will."

"Hey Krie!" He was woken by Uncle Angus.

"Ice fishing time. Get up, let's go"! Krie groaned. Sunday was supposed to be a rest day. But not here. He rolled out and put his clothes on. Haywire was already at the table. Grandmother Sopiah was sitting across from him. He had a drink of water, motioned with his head to Grandmother, and they went out for their morning prayers. She seemed weaker today, and leaned on him, swaying slightly for the duration.

"Grandmother, are you okay?"

"I just need some tea, my boy." He took it slow and easy on the way back to the house. Bonewalker leered from between the pines. Krie straightened his shoulders and looked straight ahead until he got Grandmother into her chair. When he closed the door, he ignored the Bonewalker but made it cackle when he shut the door a little too hard.

"Good to go?" Haywire was smiling.

They walked down to the road. Angus had a bounce in his walk. They took the main road to the driveway of the old cabin. Krie smelled the smoke before they got there. Haywire laughed quietly.

"Lorna musta smelt the fish cooking already."

"Thought you weren't 'sposed to talk about food before you get it."

"Good catch, Krie, sorry Grammas and Grampas." Haywire's head was toward the little graveyard.

Lorna insisted they have tea and fresh bannock before they started. Krie's stomach was terribly full but he knew already never to refuse food or drink. It was like refusing a hug from these folks.

Haywire sharpened the hatchet and axe before they started. He pulled nets out of the cache. There were two long poles leaning on the cache. Haywire attached the nets to them. Krie was curious. How on earth were they going to set nets under the ice?

"Listen to the ice, always listen carefully," Angus said.

"Yup, it's life or death." Haywire was using his quiet voice.

"Can I help?"

"Yeah, take the hatchet and chop right here." When the hole was as wide as a coffee can, Haywire handed the axe to Krie.

"Your legs cold?"

"Nope, those long-johns are like coals in the stove," Krie grinned.

He swung the axe and let it fall in the same rhythm he used when he was chopping wood. The ice had no give, unlike wood. Chips flew.

"Keep your eyes kind of slitty – you don't want a chip in them."

He did as Haywire instructed. Water sloshed into the hole.

"Good, now chop a good-sized circle." When that was done, Haywire paced out the placing of the second. He chopped this one – in half the time Krie had taken.

"Okay, you stand here. Get ready to catch the pole."

Haywire went back to the other hole, worked the pole into the water, with about a foot of it showing, and pushed it straight to Krie. He grabbed it, and worked it out his hole, leaving about a foot of the pole bobbing out. He felt the pole hit bottom and worked it a little into the bottom of the lake. The water was black in the hole.

"Okay, now we can go have tea and let the fish move in."

When they came back to check, thin ice had formed around the poles, holding them perfectly upright. They each worked one of the poles loose. Haywire gently and carefully pulled the net out. It was loaded with fish that froze as he pulled the length of the net out. Without being told, Krie fired the pole back to Haywire and then ran to the other hole to catch it. They removed the fish and filled the bin cousin Lorna had fished out of the back room.

She was grinning from ear to ear as they dropped the bin by the door. The smell of fresh fish was intoxicating. Krie ate his fill, amazed he had room for anything. It was fantastic. Uncle was smacking his lips.

The Grandmothers were thrilled when they arrived home with a couple of bins. Krie didn't mind fish again. It was fresh and delicious after weeks of meat. Later, he and Grandmother Sopiah sat at the table together, after everyone had gone to bed.

"There is a reason I have been telling you about the parts of my life I would rather not revisit, my boy."

"Why are you?"

"I want you to learn from them, as I did."

"I am not sure I understand."

"The painful things in your life, Krie, you couldn't control should never own you. They should make you strong, and make you compassionate. They should not exist in the now except to enable you to help others, to listen to others, and support others, and to stay steel strong, no matter what life throws you."

"Sort of how you described Sundance?"

"Yes, my boy. Sundance prepares you for life for the rest of the year. It isn't about the 12 days of ceremony. It is simply to prepare you for the ceremony of everyday life. You know that you have overcome suffering and hardship and you can get through anything, physical, mental, spiritual, or emotional, that life can throw you. You have Sundanced, Krie, since you were born. You carry strong medicine. You have already not allowed your past to haunt you. This is why I know you can beat the Bonewalker, and Bonewalkers to come."

"Grandmother, I wish I didn't have to."

"I know, my boy, but you have been chosen to do so."

"Why?"

"I'm not sure. Perhaps because you were born of a man who was a host of a Bonewalker and a Mother who fought one."

"Do I have a choice?"

"That is the mystery of life, my boy. We always have a choice."

"I am going to take out Mom's and Dad's Bonewalker, I can tell you." Grandmother smiled at the determination in his voice.

"I am so proud of you, Krie, for not becoming a drinker, for not letting the pain take over you."

"It's hard, Grandmother. I did drink once, and it was to get courage to talk to a girl I liked."

"How did that work for you?"

"I learned I didn't like her after all, and the hangover is something I hope I never put myself through again." Sopiah's beautiful laugh echoed through the trees.

"I will bet that you will never touch alcohol again, my boy."

"I won't, it sucks."

"How do I cope with the sensitivity, Grandmother?"

"It's your gift, you will become better at dealing with it. Try to help people with it. If you feel they are suffering, try to help them. If you feel someone is sick, tell them they can come and see Gramma Maisey."

◉◉◉

Krie told Grandmother Sopiah he was going to call the Bonewalker out.

"I'm done waiting for it, I am going to go and fight him. I am sick and tired of waiting on pins and needles for something to happen!"

"Krie, I cannot tell you what you should do. Maisey and I will be praying really hard."

Krie got his pack ready and walked toward Gramma's mountain. He remembered that spirits could hear you when you were high up. He was about to find out. It had warmed up enough to snow. It was completely silent, this vast landscape around him.

He found the trail easily enough. He took a drink from his canteen. He took a deep breath and started to climb, slowly and steadily. His feet crunched into the fresh snow, pressing his boot prints. He wondered if the snow would erase them by the time, he was making his way down, because he'd be coming down and he was determined to do so alone.

He followed Haywire's directions carefully. It took three hours before he reached the top. He stood and turned slowly to survey the distance he had climbed. He was covered in sweat. The snow had slowed. He looked to the lake and could see the Charlie cabin. He turned toward Gramma Maisey's and could see the smoke crawling out of the stovepipe. In the opposite direction, he could see Lorna's house. His family circle was tiny within a spectacular landscape. In every direction, there were mountains as far as he could see and it was all black and white, blue-tinged closer to the mountain tops, which he knew was because of the cold. He took some dry meat out of his pack, and ate it, washing it down with water. The streaks of fat were delicious, and he chewed every bit of goodness out of it as he stood.

He was ready.

"Bonewalker!" He yelled as loud as he could, in four directions.

"I'm ready for you!" He listened. There was only an echo, then silence.

The dark enveloped the cabin. There was the sound of sleep breathing from all corners. The Bonewalker had chosen a large host and was clever, stealthy. Finally, he saw the door open, and a dark figure emerged. Chuckling and quivering, the

Bonewalker crouched down. Krie was half asleep. He had needed the bathroom, and now he was unaware of anything but the need to go out to the outhouse and go back to his warm bed.

There was no warning. He felt something or someone heavy leap on him that felt like claws in his back, and before he knew it, he was on the floor and half out the door, still with his pants down. He struggled. Hot breath seared his neck. He smelled the rotten stink of it. Like something dead.

"You can't summon me; I come when I am ready." A reptilian hiss in his ear.

"Now give yourself to me." The voice was mesmerizing. Krie stopped struggling.

"That's it." His touch was horrifying, familiar. Now in his ear, "You know how much you enjoyed it before."

"*Manitou Neechiewagan*! Creator!" Krie called and began to pray loudly as he rolled out onto the snow. Bonewalker howled but came back on top of Krie. The host body was huge and strong, clearly Tlingit by his build. He appeared black, with glowing ugly eyes. He was the size of a man but had hands as big as bear paws. Krie saw Angus out of the corner of his eye. His movements became quick. He rolled hard and fast, using grappling moves he knew, and trapping Bonewalker beneath him. Like hardwood in the stove, he snapped some punches out, one after the other. He grabbed the thing by the neck. The host lay there and now felt hard like he was a giant bug shell. Krie continued to pray, this time silently. There was a hard spin, and then he was pinned under Bonewalker who was over him like a spider, long arms and legs splayed. Krie's fear rose, and he went limp.

"That's it, now you're mine." Krie heard the triumph in the voice. His head was fuzzy as if he'd been hit. Like he was drunk, and everything was in slow motion. Bonewalker gave out a low cackle, right next to his ear. Krie could hear the triumph in it and retched at the stench of fetid breath. His thoughts were tumbled, his movements slow and delayed. It was as if he had venom surging through his blood. He felt the cold under his back seep through his jacket. Weak, he gave himself over. His Grandmother Sopiah's face came before him, obliterating the Bonewalker.

"Krie," he heard her speak his name. It jolted him. His mind was clear. He felt the love within him, the love for his Grandmother, his Auntie, Mother, Gramma Maisey, Angus, Haywire, his boys. He focused all the power he had. There was a flash of light. It lit up the land like lightning, illuminating the trees, the snow, the outhouse, the cache, the cabin. And, just like that, the Bonewalker groaned, roared, and was gone.

When he stood up, Krie saw Uncle, the Grandmothers, and Haywire standing by the door of the cabin in the pale wash of moonlight. He walked to them. Each embraced him silently. When they were inside, Gramma Maisey lit the lamp. Krie felt drained, spent. The Grandmothers glanced at each other, and while Maisey made tea, Sopiah sliced and buttered bannock and cut meat up for it. They all sat, still silent, eating and sipping, with just the hissing of the old oil lamp.

"I beat him," Krie finally said. Sopiah's face looked as if it were set in stone. He knew she was very serious.

"No, sonny." Grandmother looked up. Her eyes were dark.

"Krie, that was only the First Round."

Krie's stomach tightened. What the hell was he in for?

Grandmother Sopiah and Krie prayed at dawn, despite the late night. She was walking slower than usual, and Krie was careful to help bear her weight on his arm. This was the first that he saw Grandmother cry as she prayed. He did not understand all of the Saulteaux, but tears ran as his heart was touched by the tone of her voice. It vibrated his spirit within him, and he began to cry. He sang loud and clear when it was his turn. He sang his heart out of his mouth. As they walked by the creek, Sopiah turned to him.

"Your song, my boy, your voice, is also a weapon." Krie nodded.

☉☉☉

When the silence is present, your senses are heightened. There is a waiting – waiting for the next sound, the next moment. Krie kept silent whenever he was alone. He waited for the pounce. He was on his feet like a cat, his body poised for the unexpected. And the Bonewalker did not come. One morning, Krie woke up to the drip, drip, drip of water outside the window. His nose was not cold. There was a feeling of release in the air. It was spring. Just like that. In the night, winter had walked back North and spring from the South. Krie was sad that trapping would be over, and the stillness of the land would now begin to thrive with life.

He lay for a while knowing dawn was not quite near. Bonewalker. If I can't call him, how do I set things up for the next round? It came to him. He had been alone when Bonewalker attacked.

"Uncle, can I help take the trapline down?"

"Already done, my boy."

"How did you know that it was time?"

"Felt it in my bones. Spring's' early though."

"Uncle, do you mind if I go stay down at the lake by myself over the weekend?"

"Why sure," Uncle grinned.

The Grandmothers and Haywire were silent when Krie was preparing.

"We will be here praying," Grandmother said. How had she known? Oh yes. The ancient rhythms of this land. It told him things in the breeze, the trees, the fire.

He covered miles to the lake, feeling the gravel moving beneath his boots. The air was warm on his skin and with it the fragrance of the woods in the melt. Something was following him, walking off in the bush to the right side of the road. Listening intently, he tried to determine the size of whatever it was. His feet beat a rhythm like a drum. He began to sing, softly. His heart was beating a little faster, when he sang while walking, and he shorted himself of breath. He continued. He sang for rounds of the song and started another. Grandmother's songs. They filled him the way water brims over in a glass. The sound off in the bush had gone. Oh, wait, there it was. It was as if he was being stalked. It could be a bear. It could be a lynx. And it could be a Bonewalker.

He headed down the narrow track to the cabin. Whatever was following turned with him. When he reached the door, he stopped. He listened. *It* was silent. He breathed it in for a moment and entered, bolting the door behind him. No use bear wrestling. He had other prey in mind. He was not the hunted this time. Feeling for the matches where they always were, he lit the lamp. Made fire. He put his things away and took the water pail. He let his eyes adjust to the dark then crossed to the creek and dipped the pail. He heard it then. Still to the right, whatever it was out there took one step. Sticks snapped. He breathed in, slowly, rose, and crossed back to the cabin. He heard steps, one, two, three, follow. He put the pail down by the door. Crossing back to the outhouse, he heard the sounds following him; when he was finished, and until he had moved, walking toward the cabin, there it was again.

"If it's you," he thought, "I am hunting you, not the other way around." He took the water in and had a long drink. He had never liked water but freshwater from this land was the most delicious drink there was. He removed his medicine pouch and set it on the table. He took a book from the main room and read. At first, he was listening. His plan was failing. Damn, he needed to be absorbed in the story, so that he was not in the present moment.

Hondo was narrow in the hip and broad in the shoulder, just like all Louis L'Amour's heroes. There was a beautiful woman he was sweet on. He was trying to start a new life but was an excellent shot and didn't want anyone around to know. Krie heard the creature outside, circling the cabin slowly. He listened for a moment and breathed deep. His heart beat a little faster. It was hunting him. He read, about purple canyons and brilliant sunsets. A gentle decent woman named Laura with long flowing hair and a small waist. He heard the rustling an arm's length away but did not look up. Bonewalkers didn't need to use doors? He focused as hard as he could. Hondo was about to be outed; some young and cocky gunslinger who had just recognized him.

Krie smelt the familiar stench of Bonewalker's breath.

"This body I'm in is not the one I want. The one I want is yours." Krie continued reading.

"I was in your Father. He touched you in a way a man should not touch a boy." The voice was cajoling, mocking, and creepy but different this time, a rasping whisper, low and ugly. Krie stiffened but did not look up. His breathing came faster.

"You liked it. You encouraged it. You flirted with your own Father to make it happen again.

"You liked what your Father did to you, your body liked the touch of his hand all over you. You responded like a cat." Krie felt the shame well up and tears filled his eyes. He breathed and moved his body when he read now that the hero was shot, a microsecond before the chase.

"*Laura ran to him, crying in ragged sobs, and threw himself into his arms.*"

"You like anal. You moaned as if you liked it."

Now rage came like a flame out of a deep well. Krie roared like an animal, and crying, threw himself toward the Bonewalker who simply stepped aside at the last second. Krie felt the impact of the floor and could not breathe. Could not catch his breath. He lay, sobbing uncontrollably, the memories of the cabin tore through him like gusts of gale winds. It was too much; he could not bear this. He roared again and heard screaming and crying. He realized it was him. A tidal wave of cold fear washed over him. This was not a physical fight, this was a mental battle, and he had completely given his power away.

He felt himself drowning in a pool of fear, shame, regret, a thousand feelings he could not name. It was a cold and watery hell.

"So, how about some man sex, the real thing, I mean look at my host, he's good looking enough, and I would do about anything to get myself all over you."

Krie caught his breath.

He tried to breathe deeply, but sobs tore the breath before he could. He thought of his loved ones, tried to fill his heart with love. It was not enough to erase the sick feeling that he could not name. It was no use. He lay, limp, helpless, now with the dread of what was to come. He couldn't move, could not fight this way. Why had he taken off his medicine pouch? That was it! He fought hard to sit up. The host was moving toward him, seductive, and with intent. He got off the floor. He walked to the table. His hand reached for the pouch. He put it on. The host body acted as if it had been struck by an enormous blow, and fell to the floor, like a broken bird, still. The eyes now looking up at him, with confusion, the face a mask of disbelief. Krie saw the Bonewalker in the corner. He was a huge spider-like creature, a hideous sight, with glowing eyes. He turned to face the spider.

"I planned my escape. I was terrified, but I got away from my Father. I hated what he did. If I responded to the sexual abuse, it was a natural thing that any child's body would do. Any child's skin will respond the way it's supposed to at a touch. It was something I did not even understand. I do now. I hated what was done to me. I have a volcano of rage inside me, toward my Father, but he is my Father, he brought me into this world, and it wasn't him, it was YOU!" The last word he yelled. It filled the night silence.

The host body collapsed, unconscious.

"Where in the hell am I, and who are you? How did I get here?" The host's voice was full of fear. He was an older Indigenous man, who Krie thought looked familiar. Grey-haired, without the red flush of booze. Clearly old school, as his simple bush clothes were neat and clean. He was a large man, and like most people who lived the old way, thin but obviously fit.

Krie was thoughtful. How could he answer this? He breathed in slowly and breathed out.

"You're not well. You need to go see Grandmother Maisey Charlie and ask her for help Something takes over you and you blackout."

"It happens all the time. I don't want to go to the white doctors, because they will say I'm crazy."

"I'm Krie Red Sky. I stay with the Charlie family here at Little Annie, that's where you are. We're at the old Charlie cabin just off the Carcross road. I'll walk you to it, and do you know where Grandmother Maisey's house is?"

"Yes."

"Go there now, right now. Wake them up. Tell them you were down at the cabin with me. They'll know what to do." The man pulled himself up off the floor.

"When this happens, I'm so tired after."

"I can imagine. What's your name?"

"James Abraham. My family won't talk to me. I do bad things when I am blacked out."

"Grandmother Maisey will explain. You will be able to tell them why."

"I don't think so. I hurt some kids."

The man began to cry.

"You didn't hurt kids, something else did. You need to go to Maisey, and it will all be clear to you."

"I am a bad man."

"You can change."

"No, I really did terrible things, terrible. I hate myself."

"You will feel different when you go to Grandmother's. Now let's go."

When Krie left James at the road, the moon was high. As the man sloshed through the slush and mud, he turned back around.

"Thank you."

Krie waved and prayed for James all the way back to the cabin.

Sunday morning came bright and fresh, and shining. Long before the sun, Krie had made special prayers for James, and sung all the songs he knew. When the sun was up, Krie made coffee and sat at the table. He heard a noise outside the door. There was a knock. When the door opened, there was James Abraham, head down, shoulders slumped.

"Want some coffee?"

"Yeah, and then I'm gonna walk up to the road to hitchhike back to Carcross."

"Did you get help?"

"I couldn't knock on the door. I couldn't do it. I am a dirty and bad man, and I don't deserve help."

"Everyone deserves help if they want it."

"You don't understand."

"Try me."

"I touched children wrong. Like it was done to me. I swore I would never hurt a kid after Mission School."

"That's the point, it wasn't you."

"I can't believe that."

"You have to try, it's the only way. Look, if I walk there with you, will you come with me?"

James began to cry, head on his arms on the table. It was like an animal, suffering a great and final wound. Krie waited but reached out and laid a hand on James' arm. He pulled it away as if Krie had slapped it, hard. Still, he waited. Finally, James' crying abated to sobs. He shook with them like a child, with quick intakes of breath.

"Drink your coffee. I'm going there with you. We'll do this together. It's the only chance you've got."

His voice was serious, forceful. James' head yanked up, and he regarded Krie.

"Why are you helping me, I don't deserve it."

"Because you want it. And that means you *do* deserve it."

James nodded, his face like a sad child. He sipped his coffee loudly until it was done.

"Can I have one more? It was a cold night, outside."

Krie poured another, as they sat in silence. Krie rose to pack his belongings before they headed up the trail.

When Maisey's cabin came into sight, Krie felt something was off. Haywire's truck was gone, and there was no sign of life, no telltale smoke coming out of the chimney. There was a note on the table. *Krie, I'm not feeling well so am going to Whitehorse General Hospital with Haywire and Maisey. Love always, Grandmother.*

Krie felt sick to his stomach and felt sweat trying to come out on his forehead, despite the chill of the cabin. He made fire as James sat rolling smokes. "Why the hell," he asked himself, "did I go and bait the Bonewalker when Grandmother is so ill? She could have died, and I would not have been here!"

James looked over at Krie. Krie felt his eyes and looked up.

"Why you mad?"

"Because I should have known my Grandmother was sick and come home. I should be thinking of her."

"She's almost here."

"What do you mean?"

"Almost home. Be here soon. Make tea. She'll want tea." Sure enough, Krie caught the sound of Haywire's truck. He rushed to the door.

"James,when that water boils, make the tea." He reached the truck before it stopped. Grandmother Sopiah was smiling. He gently helped her out of the truck.

"Grandmother, what happened? I was so worried."

"Oh, my boy, just that my pain was worse. I just got a different prescription, I'm okay." Krie heaved a huge sigh.

"Who came?" Maisey asked. Krie was never surprised by her knowledge.

"James Abraham."

"He will need our help. Sopiah?"

Krie could feel Grandmother's tiredness.

"Yes, of course. Maisey, just give me a few minutes to gather my things."

James was taken to the back room.

"Ho!" Haywire and Krie looked at the door at Uncle's voice. Krie got an extra cup and poured warm tea into it. He drew more water to keep hot on the back of the stove for after the healing work. Uncle came in with a blast of cool air that smelled of pine-scented forest and medicines.

"Who's here?"

"James Abraham," Haywire said knowingly. Uncle raised his eyebrows but said nothing. Krie put his tea on the table.

The Grandmothers and James were in a back room for a good deal of time. When they came out, Krie poured a fresh pot of tea.

They all sat together; James with a look of gentle peace. He nodded at Uncle, who nodded in return.

When Haywire left to fire up his truck, James shook hands all around. He addressed the Grandmothers.

"I am a bad man, but I thank you for your help."

"There is no such thing as a bad man, just a man who has let himself go off his path. Find it again. Come home to yourself, and your loved ones." He had tears in his eyes, his head down. "Choose to do good, now." Maisey was firm.

He shook hands all around again and was gone.

"Krie, what happened last night?" Maisey asked.

"Bonewalker came in James. He messed with my head." It was Sopiah's turn.

"Maisey and I have talked about how this will happen. Bonewalker has attacked you physically, and now mentally. Next two rounds will be attacking your heart and your spirit. Prepare yourself." Gramma was nodding.

"Watch. He may come in another person. Watch. Like you are hunting grizzly. Watch that grizzly doesn't hunt you." Krie nodded at Sopiah. His gut tightened. He had to be ready. He did not know how, but this wasn't anything he knew how to prepare for.

In the morning, the prayers were longer. Sopiah took her time on the walk as well.

"Krie, what did the Bonewalker say to get to you mentally?"

"He said I enjoyed being molested."

She did not speak for a long time. As they walked, holding the silence, Krie listened to the squirrels whirring their warning above. He was thinking about how all the animals help one another in these ways, when Grandmother finally spoke.

"It's a very hard thing when your body responds to someone who does not touch you with love. It is natural. People don't think of it this way, but the body is created to respond to touch and intimacy. If you responded physically, Krie, it still means it was abuse, and it still means it was not something you consented to. You know that do you?"

"For a long time, I had shame, Grandmother. It was very deep. I knew that whatever happened with my body was because a child's body is innocent, and so was I. I still am. I had to get past the anger and hurt and find that little wisdom."

"You are very wise, Krie; some people cannot get past being a victim. They stay in the hurt and then either hurt themselves or others. Being a victim is not a role, it is an experience."

"It took me a long time to get there, Grandmother. I'm still very angry at Dale Post for letting himself be taken over by Bonewalker. And I know first-hand how much damage a Bonewalker can cause. It just gave me the determination to fight and win."

Sopiah reached over and kissed his cheek.

"Krie, you are wise for your years. You'll survive anything that life throws at you, and you will save a lot of people a lot of pain. You were born to fight Bonewalkers. Maybe because you were born of a host, and a victim of a Bonewalker. You won't have it easy, Krie, but your path is an honourable one, and one most people would not be able to walk down it."

"I want one day to meet my Mother. If I beat this Bonewalker, then she will be free."

◎◎◎

The path was one Krie did not recognize, yet he felt sure of where he was going. He was heading to the meadows, but something wasn't right. As he looked up high to the mountains it looked like winter, the snow was down very low, and the mountains looked black in the frigid air above the clouds. It was milder down below, and he walked with sure feet, feeling the pack on his back. He jumped a creek and felt like he was just another animal within the silence of this wild land. A slight breeze danced across his skin. Up ahead was an opening, and then a clearing. He admired the green of the leaves and the sun illuminating them. The trees with white bark and vivid yellow leaves glowed in the sun. Rutting bull moose would be about. Bears would be looking for food. He was, for a moment, lured into admiring the shimmering beauty before him, feeling as though he was part of it and belonged in this place. It would be a good place to build a home. His eyes searched for straight trees for logs.

Too late, he felt the feeling of hair creeping up his back and neck. He slowly turned, and there stood a grizzly, standing like a man, huge paws up. It was staring at him, grunting, head swinging back and forth, back and forth. Krie's blood froze, and his guts felt loose. He looked for a tree – there was nothing tall enough. His only option was to play dead. This was going to be very, very ugly. He dropped to the ground, ensuring he was facing the huge creature and cursing for being so sure of himself that he had not brought a gun.

The bear did not move, but his head was moving back and forth even harder as he growled so deep that Krie felt it through the ground and into his very bones. God. Where were Angus and Haywire? Where exactly was he for that matter? He kept the side of his face to the ground and felt the rough grass prickling his skin. An insect tickled over his face. Still, he did not move.

From across the open, from beyond the bear, he heard a woman call his name. It was familiar and stirred something deep within; made tears come from way down deep. The bear turned its head toward the sound, sniffing the air, and grunting. Krie could smell its skunk-hot, rotten-meat breath. Then he saw her from where he lay, crossing to him and the bear. It could not be. Mother! It was Leah! She came slowly across from a grove of trees, and he and the bear watched her come.

As she moved, Krie shifted an arm beneath his head to see better. Now he could clearly see both of them. The bear was sniffing hard, and Krie knew she was still out of its range of vision. Then she was close enough, and the bear was riveted on her. No. Oh no. The grizzly roared, and still she came.

"Mother, no!" Krie shouted. But she came. She motioned Krie to stay down and walked forward directly in front of the bear. Krie could smell the powerful stink, and watched horrified as the slaver dripped from its jaws when he roared again at Leah. Krie's gut lurched, as the huge animal dropped to all fours. Its hump was enormous. His Mother walked even closer, singing what he knew was the Bear Song.

The animal stopped a few feet from her and reared up again. Krie began to sing with her, although his breath was coming in pants, his heart racing. He watched, horrified, fascinated, as she stood, fearless, directly in front of the animal. He could smell his own terror as sweat leached out of him. It smelled like metal. The bear pounced. Krie heard someone screaming and realized it was not her, but him. He could not move. The bear was mauling and smashing her with a force that was beyond what he believed a human body could take. He rose to his feet.

"No!" he screamed. "Take me!"

Ragged sobs burned his lungs, but the creature was relentless. His Mother was being thrown around like a blanket in the mouth of a dog. The bear had smashed her to the ground, again and again. Krie heard the sound of bones crunching and snapping. He sang as loud as he could. Now the animal's great jaws were around her head as if it was a small morsel. He sang louder. His horror dropped him to his knees, as he tried to run to her. At least, now he could move! So much blood. Krie's heart felt as though it would explode as he ran; it was thundering so hard and fast in his chest. The bear played with Mother as though Leah was a mouse and it was a cat. It licked blood off her head, and then Krie watched in horror while it tore her scalp back. He heard the sound of ripping cloth as her chest was laid bare and screamed again. Then his anger roared up from deep within and made his stomach fly up to his throat and burn. It had every vein boiling with blood.

"No!"

Strangely, the bear stopped, walked toward the forest, where it sat. Krie ran to his Mother. He checked her breathing, her heart. She was still alive! He tore his jacket and his shirt off. The cool air collided with the sweat on his skin, chilling him. He carefully replaced his Mother's scalp. It was hard to do it right with all the blood. Now he gently wrapped her head. Despite the fact she showed every sign of unconsciousness, she stirred.

"Krie, oh Krie, the pain, it's terrible. I knew you'd fight for me." He kissed her cheek.

"I love you Mother, with all that I am. I will kill this thing. Don't be afraid, I will get you out of this and to safety, I promise you."

"I know, my boy, I have always known."

She had tears on her cheeks but was smiling tenderly. He could see the pain in her eyes as she fainted. He gently laid her back down and covered her with his jacket. He expected to feel the paw tear the flesh of his back any second, but by some strange turn of events, the animal was leaving them both alone. He had little time, judging by the amount of blood around his Mother.

He turned. The bear's head raised and Krie ran to it in a fury, smashing as hard as he could with blows to its nose, face, and ears. The bear roared again. It reared up on its hind legs, and Krie could only land body blows to the towering creature. This was a fight for both his life and his Mother's.

The bear threw Krie with an enormous paw. He felt huge claws tear across his back as he rolled hard across the grass. The wind was knocked out of him. Now he felt real fear, knowing he was utterly vulnerable. He heard it circling, the weight of it snapping logs so loud with each step that it was like the deafening crack of gunshots. Krie caught his breath and heaved again, and again. The bear was in sight and facing him, circling like a man. Then the bear turned completely away, and when it turned back it was a man. It was his Father. It was Dale Post.

Post leered at Krie. Krie saw the ugliness in the eyes.

"Your Mother loved it when I fucked her." Krie heard her moan from where she was.

"She was ashamed and told people I raped her. It wasn't true. Your Mother is a common whore. She loved it rough and the kinkier the better." He threw back his head and laughed. The sound chilled Krie to his bones. Krie spoke now, and his voice was low, deep, and quiet.

"I am going to kill you."

Post laughed again, and was taunting when he replied,

"Oh, you think so?" There are different ways of killing. I killed your Mother's spirit. That's better than taking their life, because it's the same, it's just the misery you have to live with.

"I am going to kill you. "Krie was shouting now, his voice echoing. He heard it come back off the mountains – *kill you, kill you.*

"You are not allowed to harm a hair on the head of a relative. You should know that."

"Oh, now you're cultural," Krie spat these words with the fury that was boiling in him.

Krie fell to his knees and vomited. Dale Post laughed – a dry, ugly, laugh, long, and hard. It rang in Krie's ears. His hand felt for what he prayed was there. And then there it was. A rock. He grasped it, rose, and ran like a shot to Post. He smashed his twisted face as a gash opened and blood spilled. Post staggered. Krie aimed for Post's skull. There was a loud crack.

"Fuck!" Post yelled, "You two assholes and the head wounds, fuck!" His hand went to his head where blood poured brutally. His eyes rolled back in his head and he dropped in slow motion to the ground. Still. Lifeless. Krie bolted toward his Mother. She had vanished.

Krie stood in disbelief. There was the grass, crushed from where his Mother had lain but there was no blood. His eyes scanned the entire meadow. Nothing. His Father. Oh God, he had killed his own Father! His heart ached as he faced the truth of his actions. He had broken a sacred promise. Not to harm a relative. Tears came and ran with the sweat down his face. Confused, he spun to face where Dale Post was and ran back to him. There was no sign of him. There was something – a set of 10 grizzly claws lay in a neat pile. Dazed, he picked them up, one by one.

He did not know how but had made it home. He had no notion of the time it had taken for him to get there. When Krie stood in the doorway, the Grammas quickly rose to their feet, Uncle and Haywire were nowhere to be seen.

"Krie, are you alright?" His face was frozen, he was as white as a sheet and covered with sweat.

He fell into a chair, while Maisey got tea. Though he didn't take it, she loaded it with a great deal of sugar and demanded he drink. As he sipped, the life came back into him. The shock and feeling of being stunned retreated like a slinking wolf.

He told them all that had occurred. Their faces fell and tears flowed. He knew his recounting was absurd, but neither said a word.

When he was done, they sat in silence. Maisey was the first to speak.

"Sonny, that was Bonewalker."

Krie felt sweat break out on his forehead as nausea rose. Sophia added,

"Round Three, Krie, that was the heart round. He went for your greatest emotional wounds – the harm and loss of your Mother as a baby."

Krie could only shake his head.

"I almost didn't get through it," he said quietly. Maisey's voice was firm.

"But my boy, you *did*."

Krie needed to think, and he needed to prepare. He did not need to be told Round Four was going to be the toughest. After prayers, he slept again and when he rose, Haywire and Angus were there.

"Krie, you did it," said Haywire.

"What we couldn't," agreed Uncle.

"Pray for me. Round Four is going to be the worst of them. I can feel it in every cell of my being. I need your prayers." The men nodded.

"Feel like a drive to Carcross?" Haywire asked. "I need to visit Uncle Charlie."

"No, I think I will go down to the old cabin. I need to be alone." The men exchanged glances.

"Watch your back." Haywire was serious.

"Remember everything we have taught you."

Krie nodded, determined.

◎◎◎

Sopiah was fading. Krie could see how she was losing her colour, had a greyish tone, and her movements were slower. She was so thin. The walks by the creek were shorter. He felt sad as he saw her dwindle but her spirit seemed stronger, somehow. One early morning after prayers, Grandmother asked him what was on his mind.

"You look so weak, Grandmother, so frail."

"It won't be long now for me, Krie, but I am where I want to be. Right here, with you, with Maisey, and with Haywire, and with Angus.

"Grandmother, how did you first meet Gramma Maisey and Angus?" She was silent for a time; he waited.

"They were the ones who saved me. Angus was the one who swam that lake with me, and Maisey nursed me back to health." Krie could not speak.

"Grandmother, Angus has Sundance scars?"

"Yes, my boy. He was drawn to Manitoba because he wanted to connect with the culture of our mutual ancestors. He started dancing with our people. He danced for many years, prayed for many people. He is a Healer in his own right."

"He doctors with words and by teaching."

"Yes. He carries a great deal of knowledge. He always was a very humble man."

"You still love him." She sighed long and deep.

"Yes, my boy, I always have. I never got over him. He never married. I know it was because he couldn't love anyone like he knew I loved him. He chose aloneness. It was how he honoured my love. And I have honoured his by sending you to this family and making you safe. And, I have come to die with these ones who gave me life."

"Grandmother, I am afraid for you to die."

"Why, my boy?"

"I don't want to have to walk this world without you."

"My boy, I understand. But this is something you will have to learn to do."

"That and beat the Bonewalker."

"Yes, and beat the Bonewalkers." He did not miss the "s" on the end of her last word.

"Take this. It's been around my neck since it was given to me. Don't ever take this off. And my medicine bundle here, this is yours now, and you know how to use it. That's right, you hold that like a baby. It's all a bone game, my boy. It's partly about guessing, part luck. You can't let things distract you, or make you take a wrong turn. Bonewalkers will do anything to take control. Remember that first game you played, and the other team did all they could to distract you from guessing the bones? Boy, they sang and drummed and made their dance all to distract you from guessing the bones! Life will do the same, and so will the 'other.' Don't allow your focus to be disturbed. Never let your enemy distract you. Like any other bone game, it's about gambling, guessing, focus, and chance. You have to take risks to play, that is how you must play in life. Winning the bone game against a Bonewalker is life and death. If you win against that darkness, you have won the bone games. You are going to send that Bonewalker to the place in between where it can never harm anyone again. You have it in you, I've always known this."

The moon illuminates her face. Her smile is weak, but her almost closed eyes are glowing, and he feels the pang in his heart, where that glow reaches.

"I'm going to sleep now, my boy. I'm so tired."

He was not ready to walk this earth without her. The ground felt unsteady. He prayed, hard. He held her hand; he did not let it go even hours later when she breathed her one last sweet breath. One small, sweet sigh. One inhale she was here in this world, and with the next exhale she was forever gone from it. A bolt of energy shot through him like an electric shock. He held her words so tightly as if the words were the hand in his. He willed himself to remember them, always. Later, he sat with her hand in his; her bundle next to his heart.

◉◉◉

This is where they found Krie before dawn. There would be no dawn prayer today, he had cried them out all night. Grandmother lay, dignified, just as if she had fallen asleep.

Gramma Maisey was the one who asked Uncle to bless the grave site. Uncle had tears in his eyes but nodded. She asked Haywire to dig the grave. Haywire was silent. He sat at the table drinking coffee, the smoke from his cigarette slowly curling up from his hand. He shook his head slowly, rose and left the cabin. Krie knew he had gone to be with Angus. He felt lost. Gramma Maisey shooed him out of the back room.

"I gonna help prepare her, you can't be here. Women's ways are not for men to see."

Krie sighed and walked slowly up the hill to the graveyard. Angus was sobbing in Haywire's arms. He heard his voice as he entered through the little fence.

"I loved her, the wife of my heart. I only ever wanted *her*. And now she is gone from me."

"At least until you go to her, Uncle." Haywire's voice was gentle. It was his turn to break down. He shook in Uncle's arms. Krie sighed, picked up the shovel where Angus had dropped it and began to dig. The sweat poured from his face, neck, chest, and back, but still, he dug. He sang. It was a song of prayer. He used the shovel as his drum. The throwing of the dirt was his rattle. He dug until the hole was over his head.

"I need help."

Haywire and Uncle pulled him out.

Angus and Haywire had an old door covered with a blanket. They gently placed Grandmother on it, and carefully raised it up. They slowly made their way out of the cabin and up the hill, Gramma and Krie behind them. When they reached the top, a large eagle sat in the tree just above. There it stayed as they said their prayers. There it stayed when the men used ropes to gently lower Grandmother's blanket-wrapped body in the ground. Krie grasped the shovel.

He began the same song, using the shovel as his drum, and the sound of the dirt landing as the counter-rhythm. He sang until the hole was filled. Haywire had a wooden marker. On it was "Sopiah Red Sky." Krie wondered when he'd had the time to carve it, but in the twilight he saw that it had a beautiful scene. It was Little Annie Lake, with Gramma's mountain showing across the water. Haywire put the marker at her head and tamped the earth to keep it upright. Now Krie was forever part of this land.

Krie sat in wonder. In the dark, his eyes adjusted, and he saw Gramma Maisey sitting at his feet. To his left was Uncle, to his right was Haywire. He did not have to ask who was at his back, to the West. He knew it was his beloved Grandmother. Her power had come to him, and he knew as sure as the sun would rise soon, that it would never leave.

A dragonfly flew around a circle of animals. A hummingbird buzzed by. What was a hummingbird doing this far North? He watched it dart and buzz until it landed on the bear's head! There were rabbits, gophers, and even mice until the large circle was full, and the air full of the winged ones. He stood, entranced, looking at each creature. The flying ones left shimmers of iridescent colour and light in a wake of energy. He watched as the golds, blues, pinks, and turquoises of the dragonfly were left in the air behind its flight path like a memory. It was the same as the hummingbird. Exquisite colour trails of energy and light behind them as they moved. He slowly turned, looking at all these wild things that stayed with him. He saw the glow of energy, felt it surging throughout his being. He was filled with a glowing sense of beauty, of peace.

He stood, eyes closed, and slowly turned, reaching out his hands in front of him. He felt the power enter his being, and he did not resist. The power of all these creatures and the spirit of them flowed through him, a river of being. It flowed with the direction of his blood, through his heart, and throughout his body. Then he heard it. A snarl, a low terrible growl. He froze and waited. There was the smell before he saw it. It was the size of a small dog and shaped like a bear – a pair of yellowish bands running from shoulder to rump, large head with a short, stout neck. Its head and tail were low while it moved to him, walking with an arched back. The stench of it was familiar. It choked Krie.

As it drew closer, he felt as though his chest was being squeezed, and his breath was short. The energy of power from all the creatures was gone, replaced now by fear. He watched as the other creatures shimmered and half disappeared ghostlike. As it stared, he saw and felt the wickedness of the creature. The squeezing of his chest was terrible now, and he could barely pull in a breath. Overcome with weakness and vertigo, Krie fell over. He felt as though he was being held down and turned his face to the creature whose fetid reek was overpowering.

The creature circled Krie. As it moved, he felt a paralysis, as if every muscle was in spasm. Now dizzy from lack of oxygen,

Krie felt helpless, wracked by the knowledge that he could not fight this, that the creature had power greater than he would ever have. He closed his eyes. His mind was clouded, he tried to pray but could not find words. He wanted to sing a power song but could not get his voice to obey. It came out in a weak frog-like croak. This was it. This was how he was going to die, and there was nothing he could do.

There was an enormous flash. Had lightning struck very near? Krie felt an impact to his left. Now able to move his head, he looked in that direction. The wolverine lay motionless. Krie pulled himself up. Now the thing was translucent, melting. He looked beyond to the arc of creatures at his sides and to his front. They appeared now as before, in shimmering beauty. He felt that beauty and power flowing through him again. It was done. ·

Krie told the story of the dream. When he had finished, Gramma, Uncle, and Haywire sat in the silence that was, for his family, not a silence. He felt their love within it, their respect, their gratitude. There was no need for words. They all knew that he had defeated the Bonewalker; that he was now and forever in the in-between.

◉◉◉

It was the hardest thing Krie had ever had to do when he boarded the plane. He wanted to run back across the tarmac and go back to Little Annie where he belonged. He turned and waved to Haywire and Uncle who were leaning on a fence that enclosed the runway from the parking lot. They both waved back, and Krie's eyes filled with tears. He would never forgive himself if Uncle had left forever before he returned.

"One year," he said to himself. "I will do what I need to do in one year. Then come home." His throat and chest were aching with leaving, more so than with the excitement of going. He allowed himself to feel this, knowing that it would pass, and grow to be missing those he loved. Letters. He would have to write letters; there was no phone service or internet. They'd like that. He'd write home every week.

Krie woke, looked out the window into the night. The plane was coming in for its final approach, and he could see lights glinting right to the horizon. He thought of the mountains back home, how if one climbed to the top of one, all there was to see were more peaks as far as the eyes could see. Here it was lights. His heart beat a little faster as he wondered how he was going to adjust, find his way around, find work. He breathed and remembered what Uncle had said: "Everything will be there waiting for you, just like game on a hunt. It is there for you to find."

"I wonder," Krie thought to himself, "is there a someone waiting for me, too?"

He was overwhelmed from the minute he set foot in the airport. Crowds of people, noise, light, movement everywhere. There was no break in this crazy, urban jazz soundtrack of all the senses. By Friday night, he felt as though his nerves were raw from the constant stimulation. When a loud siren on a huge firetruck went by him on the street, he covered his ears. How did people live with this? He ached for the silence of the bush. He stayed in his room that night at the hostel. He started a letter home.

Dear Uncle Angus and Haywire, and anyone else who reads this,

My first week has been hard. Boy, there is way too much noise here, and my ears are always searching for the silence that isn't there. Like the bush there is alive with creatures, here in the city it is alive with people. There is a large number who have run into hard times. Folks here give them spare change, but I can't help but think that how we all look after each other up there would be a good thing here. It's hard to walk by those who look hungry. It's a little dangerous to walk, though. The first day I almost got hit four times in four blocks, because traffic does not slow or stop for pedestrians. I was pulled back four times just in time. There are no trees in the new downtown. You have to go to parks to find them, and they are skinny and small. But you ought to see the subway! It is an underground passenger train with little malls along the lines. Handy for people in the winter, I'll bet. On the upside, the city is beautiful in its own way. The old city by the river is fun to walk around because the streets are narrow, and the buildings make you feel as though you are in France or something. The modern city sits side-by-side with the old, and is all towers of glass, and down below lights, and traffic. They are like square, tall mountains. I can't see the tops of some of them from the street! I got a room in a house right away with an older lady. She is French and Métis, and refuses to speak English. Her name is Madame Brodeur. I wish I took French, although it's like this French is Tlingit, and the French in school is Tahltan. I am having to learn this language. The landlady feeds me as though I haven't ever eaten. I am going to get fat for sure. She told me to go to the Native Friendship Centre of Montreal; she said they got all kinds of connections there. So that is the plan first thing Monday. To learn the transit system before winter, and to get a job. I don't jump from the traffic noise I wear my headphones and play my music. I was told the ice storms are terrible. I kind of wish there was an ice storm now! It's hot. Hot and humid and sweat pours off me because I am so used to the dry up there. And I miss it! I miss you two, and Gramma Maisey, Doris, and Lorna. I miss being able to pray by the water. It's not the same by a window looking out to other houses. I have to pray harder to feel anything. So that's it so far. I have one friend, the landlady, Mme. Brodeur. Mme. is short for Madame. She pretends to be annoyed when I speak English but judging by the twinkle in her eyes that reminds me of Grandmother Sopiah, she's actually trying to help me learn to speak Québécois (Quebec French). Wish me luck, this weekend I am going to force myself out into the noise and go to some of the whole bunch of free festivals around. If I can't avoid the noise, I may as well distract myself. I love you both and miss you. It aches like a toothache.

Love, Krie

Dear Krie,

We were happy to get your letter and know that you are o.k. Angus was sure that you would end up in Hong Kong! Be careful with yourself. Don't let one of those drivers catch up to you, we need you around. Your landlady sounds like my mother! She's doing better, she got sick for a long while, but the doctors say there is no sign of cancer, so she is back in her house and raising hell all over the place, so she must be better. I ran into your pal there in Carcross, that Albert Ross. Here he was, working at the cafe, pumping gas. And you will never guess who is working right alongside him, helping him away. Ben Abraham! He takes the money, and Albert does the gas pumping. They were laughing together and having a great time. I thought you would be happy to hear that. It surprised me; I can tell you! Uncle is making lynx stretchers here, grumbling about how the changes in how the land is makes it harder to set them. He is determined to get some lynx. I think it's a matter of pride, because they are harder to catch. Here's hoping. Oh, and I forgot to say we had a visit from James Abraham a week back. He is back on the land, has been since you met up with him down at the cabin. He quit drinking and is living like us. He looked happy and peaceful. I bet the whole of Carcross is glad for that, because he was a fighter. Me, I'm thinking that a year is a long time, and hope that you still come home then. I get worried that city life might pull you in, and you may not find home exciting enough after. But we know it's your life, and it's for you to choose. We just miss having you home. It's not the same without you. Uncle keeps saying "I wonder what Krie is doing now." It's driving me nuts. Mom said to say hi, and so did Lorna, and Gramma Maisey. Lorna's taken up with some German guy who came to hunt and decided not to go home. He's a good guy, likes how we live, and is full of questions about how we do things. He makes her really happy – this week!

Us too, she is always baking something, so we have a lot of cookies and cakes which is kind of nice. Anyways, take really good care of yourself so you come home in one piece. You said you miss us like a toothache. For us it is more like missing an arm. We love you.

Haywire and Uncle Angus

Krie cried as he read his letter. His heart ached for home, his stomach wanted wild meat, and he wanted to smell the clean

air and drink the pure water of home. He wanted to see Angus'
green back ahead of him as they walked the land, and know
Haywire had his back. Being away was harder than he ever
imagined.

The Native Friendship Centre of Montreal felt much more like
home. As soon as Krie saw the logo on the window in front of
the building, he felt better. Walking through the doors, he saw
his people and smiling friendly faces. Folks took the time to ask
where you were from, to visit, to have coffee and just be. His
appointment was at 2, and he was happy he was early, it gave
him an opportunity to look around and meet some people. A
circle of people in the main reception area looked like a gang
of city crows. They were visiting and drinking coffee and
laughing. They were from all over the place. Krie picked up
some program pamphlets and started to read. The Centre had
a lot of services, including a youth drop-in center. That would
be a good place to make some friends. Ka'wahse Street Patrol
was seeking volunteers. Krie brightened up. Now, this was
something that would be worthwhile. He went to the receptionist and waited for her to have a moment between calls. She
smiled up at Krie.

"What can I do for you?"

"I'm interested in talking to the Ka'wahse Street Patrol
Team Leader. I'd like to volunteer."

"Fantastic, they always need volunteers. Most people give it
up after the first few nights. You see some pretty rough stuff."

"Well, I'm not really a quitter."

"Okay, give me a minute to give the Team Lead a call."
Krie sat down next to a young man about his age who was

Inuit, judging by the copper skin, high cheekbones, and broad, genuine grin. Krie had seen Inuit in the Yukon where they would drive down the Ice Road from Inuvik to buy trucks.

"You're Inuit?"

"Inna what?" The man and Krie both laughed.

He was dressed head to toe in denim. His thick, black hair was long.

"Yeah, I'm George. Where you from?"

That was a question Krie learned he would get a lot of. White people always asked, "What do you do?" and Indians were always interested in who you were and where you came from.

"Came from the Yukon, but I'm a mutt. Cree on my Father's side, and Salteaux and Salish on my Mother's side, with a whole bunch of other stuff thrown in there."

"Sounds like some stories there."

"Oh, *yeah*. You have no idea!"

George led the way to the Elders' Lounge. It had comfortable-looking couches and a couple of Elders sitting, chatting. Krie walked straight up and shook hands with the first of three elderly ladies and an elderly man.

He saw a young man enter and felt him watching him carefully. Krie turned and smiled.

"Hi, I'm Krie Red Sky."

"Hi, I'm Gerry, Team Lead for the Street Patrol."

"Do you know George?" George and Gerry nodded to one another, the up-chin nod. Krie grinned. "What do you know?" he thought. "They do that here, too!

"I'll just get you to fill out this form, and sign it, then you can start patrolling with us tonight. We head out at 8. Okay with late nights?"

George regarded Krie seriously.

"Man, you sure you wanna do that? It's hard out there on the street, there's a lot of ugliness and pain. You look like a guy who has never seen that."

"I've lived it. I am okay, but thanks!"

George slowly shook his head. "Well, you're a better man than I!"

Then, Krie heard a voice. A beautiful melodic woman's voice. It was ringing with laughter and coming toward them. A face appeared in the doorway and Krie's heart stopped.

She was drop-dead gorgeous, and she was looking straight at him. He stared, speechless. She seemed unaware of her impact, and simply said, "Krie Red Sky?"

"Yeah, yes, um yeah." George slugged him on the arm gently and laughed. Krie felt the heat of the blush that crept up his neck to his ears and face. He felt like brake lights. George was still looking at him, giggling. Krie shot him a look, and George laughed harder.

"Hi, I am Sequoia Waabigiizhig. I'm the Employment Coordinator. I know we were supposed to meet at 2, but the receptionist said you were too good looking for me to wait that long." She was teasing, but Krie blushed harder. George was leaning over; he was laughing so hard.

"Um, so, um, do you have time right now to meet?"

"For sure, follow me."

When she sat down opposite, her black eyes were soft, but there was a twinkle of mischief in them. "God," he thought, "I am done for."

Krie sat staring at Sequoia unable to speak. He couldn't take his eyes off her. Her eyes were twinkling.

"So, where you from, Krie, clearly Cree, right?"

"Ye— yeah, my first name is a dead giveaway, right?" He felt awkward and unsure of himself. His voice sounded goofy in his head.

"Northern Cree? The men are generally as pretty as the women."

Krie flushed, again, from his neck up. He felt like an idiot.

"Uh-yeah, so my Father was Cree, my Mother is a blend, Saulteaux, and Salish, with a Tlingit-Tagish connection from the Yukon."

"Wow. Well, your ancestors got around. And that makes you really interesting." She was grinning wickedly at him. What the hell was he supposed to say? She was playing with him and he liked it, but he did not know how to play back. Now he felt downright stupid.

"So, about a job?" She was still smiling.

"Right down to business, hey," he thought.

"Uh, well, uh, I just got here to Montreal from the Yukon, and I need a way to feed myself." He was focusing on how he was going to make sure that happened.

"So, what experience have you got then?" She put on glasses that made her even more adorable. He looked at her smooth, dark skin, the large eyes, which were regarding him seriously now, her upturned nose, high cheekbones, and long thick black hair. He knew what he wanted alright, but now a job was the furthest thing from his mind.

"Oh man," he thought, "I am in some big trouble."

He didn't know how it all happened, but by the time he left Sequoia's office, he had a job interview with the Elders' Coordinator at the Centre and her phone number. He hadn't asked for it. She had passed it to him and said,

"Make sure you get a job, good lookin'. I can't date clients. Here is my number for when you land one. Make sure you call. You are so pretty I could try my jingle dress on you and send you out on the Powwow arbour and nobody would suspect a thing." He laughed at the thought.

He liked how she teased him. Her smile, and the gentle way she teased a laugh out of him. He felt awkward and at the same time as though a million dollars had just dropped in his lap.

He shook her hand, thanked her and carefully placed her number in his wallet. Things were looking up.

The interview went great. The panel members were looking intently at him.

Ms. Kristine Linklater, the Executive Director, was smiling at him the entire time.

"I heard you have a way with the Elders."

"Well, I was taught to take care of them and to really respect what they know."

"It was noticed, Krie, by the Street Team Lead, and that is why we chose to shortlist you right away. It's not about experience, it's about how you treat the Elders, and we know already from the staff that you were extraordinarily kind to them."

"Well, thank you. I have one year here before I head back home. I want to be honest so that you know that is my plan."

"Well, we appreciate that, Krie, and you will be hearing from us, no later than tomorrow afternoon."

"As long as it doesn't interfere with my street patrolling."

"We'll make sure that it doesn't."

He walked out of the boardroom with a bounce in his step, whistling. Things were going to be okay. Things were going to be very okay.

Krie was surprised to get the call from the Executive Director; It had only been three hours.

"Mr. Red Sky, Ms. Linklater speaking. The Native Friendship Centre of Montreal would be pleased to offer you the position of Elders Coordinator, starting next Monday morning. The panel was unanimous. Would you like to accept the position?"

"Would I ever!" Krie was over the moon. Not only would he have an income, he would have a valid excuse to see Sequoia every day!

Krie woke on Monday morning, as always, missing Grandmother, Gramma Maisey, Uncle and Haywire. At least he would be able to pour his missing them into taking care of Elders now. He was excited to start, and more excited to see Sequoia. He was disappointed to find Sequoia was out all week for training.

Dear Haywire and Uncle Angus

I am happy to say I got a job; I am the Elders' Coordinator for the Native Friendship Centre of Montreal. I love the Elders; they are such a blast to be with. At night, I've been volunteering out with the Street Patrol people. It was hard to see the suffering out there, from at-risk youth to Elders, people struggling. Cities and our people are not really good for each other, it seems.

I'm going to cut the volunteer work down to Friday nights, because there is a lot to do in my day job, and I need energy for all these Elders! There's so much they want to do! I made a good friend, an Inuk from Inuvik. He wants to get home eventually but is here until he raises the money to fly. Maybe he and I will drive back next July. You'd like him. He makes me laugh. I also met a girl. I think she likes me but am sort of not sure. She's a good woman. I've been told she's VERY traditional. I hope that she is because I would like to bring her home for you to meet. I think you'd like her. I don't feel like I communicate well with her yet but hope to. I'm trying to get up the courage to ask her out. She gave me her number, so I think she wants me to. I sure hope so!!! Anyway, that's about it, just busy with work and stuff. I'm socking money away for the trip home next July and to pay both of you back for the money you lent me to get here. Thank you for that, I should be able to pay you back by first payday, at least part of it. I love you guys. Please visit Grandmother's grave and tell her how much I miss her. I miss you two guys too, every day, and you are in my prayers each morning. It doesn't make up for seeing you, but it helps!

Love, Krie

Dear Krie,

Uncle wants you to know that you're in deep trouble by the sounds of it. He thinks you've already given your heart away. He keeps shaking his head and saying "There he goes." It's pretty funny. The boys are doing good, they are excited to start kindergarten and grade one, although it's still only August. They made me drive by the school in Carcross the other day, and at least this year are happy to be going. Let's see how they are after the first week of getting up early!

Uncle is slowing down a bit, I don't know what's going on, but I notice that he isn't as spry as usual. Nothing to worry about, but I am keeping an eye on it.

I saw Ben and his sidekick Albert. They have started a little food stand and are making money hand over fist off the tourist buses. Some bannock stuff, all kinds. The tourists love it. It's good to see. Ben Abraham stopped in not too long ago. He came with a brand new .30.30 for you, as a gift. I'll keep it for when you get home. He gave us all gifts for helping him as he says, "straighten out." Geez, I guess if he can do it, there is help for me, yet!

Big news. Heard your Mom is doing better, so much that she's out of the hospital. She ran into my second cousin down South, and she said she had a good chance at a government job. I wish the best for her but think we all should hold off contacting her until the time is right. I thought you would want to know.

As for us, it's the same old same old. Nothing changes, but I kind of like it that way. And I'm glad it's only 11 months until you get back here, we need your big mug around. Oh, thanks for the money, we can always use it.

Love, Haywire and Uncle Angus

Krie was into week two when he heard the voice that made his blood race and his heart sing.

"Sequoia, you look beautiful. How was the training session?"

"Good, only would have been better with you there." She was smiling frankly at him. He wondered if he would ever get used to her being so honest.

"Well, I was wondering if you would like to meet for lunch today?"

"I was thinking dinner." Krie blushed. Damn, he wished she didn't make him feel like a little kid. She laughed.

"I'm glad you blush around me that means you like me, and that is a really good thing because I like you right back!!"

Krie couldn't wait for the day to be over. He grabbed a bike for volunteers at the Centre and rode home as hard as he could. He dressed in his best clothes and boots. Mme. Brodeur wolf-whistled at him and winked as he opened the front door to leave. He made his way back downtown but was careful not to peddle too hard and break out in a sweat. It didn't work. The damned humidity got him, and he was slick by the time he reached their meeting place. Sequoia was out front, waiting, in a white dress. She looked more beautiful, her cappuccino skin glowing against the white. She was on her cell. Her brow was furrowed, and she had high-colour in her cheeks.

"I'm going to need you to hold to your promise, you said this would be done already, and you haven't done a thing." Pause. He heard a man's voice through her phone when he drew close. She flashed him a brilliant smile with a "one minute" sign.

"Bruce McNevin, I need you to take care of this, no more stalling. I'm holding you to your promise, and I am *done* being patient. Please get this done." Before she hung up, Krie could hear the man's voice, still speaking. She turned off her phone, put it in her bag, and took Krie's arm.

"I'm starving, are you starving?" He could only nod as they walked into the restaurant.

He was subdued when they sat, wondering if she had a boyfriend nobody knew about? He was feeling a little less sure of himself. He couldn't ask.

"Krie, you seem a little distracted."

"That phone call seemed to upset you."

"It did but now we are here, and I want to enjoy it."

"Fair enough. But just so you know, if you ever need to talk about it, I am a good listener."

"I know," she gently touched his hand. Her touch went through him like a fire. He started trembling and hoped she did not notice.

"Do you like sushi?"

"I've never had it."

"Oh, yeah, I guess Yukon isn't exactly swimming in sushi bars," she giggled, and he smiled widely.

"Nope, and I am a bush Indian, so raw fish isn't in the cards."

"I know what you mean. Traditionalists think raw fish is for the Inuit only."

"Yeah, we have the simple everything-has-to-be-cooked-to-a-second-death rule." She laughed, hard, holding her stomach.

"You have such a funny way of saying things, thanks, I need that laugh." He stopped trembling. This was going to be okay. He just needed to breathe, relax.

"I know who you are, you know."

"You do?" Krie had no idea what she meant.

"Yeah. You know about Bonewalkers, don't you?"

Krie choked on his tea. Sequoia had to come over and pat Krie on the back for a few minutes until he could catch his breath. Because the tea went down the wrong way, he could barely croak out the words.

"You know about Bonewalkers?"

"Yes, unfortunately. I am one who was chosen to fight them, and you were too."

"How — how?"

"How did I know? Because my Grandmother told me."

"But I've never met your Grandmother."

"She told me a long time ago I would meet you." Krie could still barely breathe without coughing.

"She did?"

"Yes, your spirit name is 'Bear Child,' isn't it?"

"Yes," Krie could only stare at her.

"Thank *God*!"

Krie looked at her quizzically.

"She told me your spirit name, how you looked, where you were from, she told me how I would meet you, and how I would feel the first time I laid eyes on you. And she told me you were one who fights the 'others.' There is more, but I am not entirely sure how you would take the news."

"Try me," Krie had found his voice.

"Well, it's awkward to say, so I will just blurt it."

"Okay."

"You and I are going to get married, and we'll have a child. The child is going to be the most powerful Bonewalker warrior the world has ever seen."

Krie started coughing again.

"Umm …"

"Yeah, I know, you don't know what to say. Look, this is hard for me too, I mean this is like the ultimate arranged marriage."

Despite himself, Krie began laughing.

"This is going to take me some time to mull over. Don't get me wrong, you're beautiful, and I feel like an idiot around you, awkward … like a kid."

"You take all the time you need. It's big news, I know. My Grandmother said you would say that, too."

"Well, maybe you should tell me all the other stuff I'm going to say and save me some work."

She threw her head back and laughed long and hard.

"She said you would really make me laugh."

"You do the same for me."

She smiled at him. He felt from his core to his skin that smile heating him in a way he had never experienced before. He wanted to be with this woman more than anything he had ever wanted before. But he would have to tell her his story first. That was going to be very, very hard.

⊚⊚⊚

There was a knife edge to Sequoia's voice as it cut through the open door of her office.

"Bruce McNevin is my husband, that is correct." Krie's head was full of buzzing, and he missed the rest. She looked up, startled. The blood had drained from his Krie's face as he stood, unable to utter a word.

Sequoia caught up with him as he was unlocking his door. "Let me explain."

"I have an Elders' Council meeting. I can't make them wait."

"Look, you don't understand, he isn't ..." She saw the look on Krie's face. It was stone.

"Rough day, sonny?" It was Gladys. How had he not heard her walker?

"Yeah, I was getting married one minute and the next she has a husband."

"I don't unnerstan."

"That makes two of us."

"Well, you and I need to go to Social Services tomorrow. The bastards took my grandkids into care."

Krie sank his head into his arms.

"No. No. What next?"

Gladys and Krie made it to the Social Services office on time. He had been sweating his way through the traffic, thinking it would not help Gladys if they kept government people waiting. It was a typical government office. Gladys snorted when she saw the "Aboriginal Services" sign.

"Aboriginal Services, my foot. The only service they provide is taking our kids into care."

"Gladys, I know you're upset. I know that you're worried. Try to focus on fighting for the kids, okay?"

"Yeah, sonny; never know. We may be dealing with actual humans."

"I hope so." Krie was worried about those kids too, and the Mom. It wasn't her fault she had to work to feed her family.

They were kept waiting half an hour. This didn't help Gladys' mood any.

Finally, her name was called.

"You come too, sonny," and then under her breath she said, "Maybe you can hold me back from crawling across the table and choking them!"

They entered a small interview office. Krie was prepared with a notepad and pen. He was sure if he was in Gladys' position, he would not grasp the whole conversation.

"Well, Mrs. Henry, I understand you are the Grandmother of Josh, Lena and little Charlie, is that right?"

"Yes, and I am here to say I am willing to take them if they can't go back to their Mother."

"Well, your daughter is actively engaged as a sex worker again, so that's not going to happen until she gets out." Gladys' face froze. Tears came to her eyes, and her jaw tightened.

"You have it wrong. My daughter works, she does books for the Cash and Carry!"

"She did up until seven months ago, Mrs. Henry, and she got back into the street trade when she lost her job." Gladys looked as though someone had slapped her in the face. Krie felt sick to his stomach.

"I don't believe it."

"I am sorry, Mrs. Henry, but she has a recent police record for soliciting."

"I want to take my grandchildren; they can live with me." Krie was amazed. Love was something. How on earth, was this bone-thin, old girl with a walker going to manage three active children under five?

"We do place children with family when possible. Is there someone who can help you with their care?"

"Yeah, him," Gladys pointed to Krie. He knew he bloody well had to. He nodded,

"You and I are going to the Housing Coordinator as soon as we are back at the Centre. I will introduce you and explain the situation. We're going to take care of those grandkids of yours, somehow."

Glady's smiled, her face softening. Krie looked at her, and said, "Believe it."

"I do, sonny, you are pretty convincing." "God," Krie thought, "I sure hope I can pull this off!"

After working with all the housing agencies, he could find, and hitting roadblocks to housing in the time frame needed for Gladys to get her grandchildren, Krie thought of Mme. Brodeur. Gladys and he had somehow convinced Mme. Brodeur to open her five-bedroom home to both Gladys and the children. Krie felt like he was on top of the world. Now the real work would begin. Two weeks in Montreal, and he was going to be a foster Dad.

◎◎◎

The second meeting of the Elders' Council was a hot one. There was much discussion about how to raise money, and what to use it for.

The council was elected from the Elders' group, which numbered over 100. The council was 12 individuals chosen for their leadership skills and ability to voice the needs of the Elders of Montreal. According to the files, they ranged in age from 65 to 92. Not all 12 were present, but they had a quorum of seven. They were as diverse a group of Natives as could be. Men and women, from all across Turtle Island. There were Inuk, Cree, Anishinaabeg, Huron. Some had been urban their entire lives, and some were bush Indians who had landed here by no choice of their own.

They were all very passionate, so the discussion was a lively one, but not at first.

"Lily, what do you think? You haven't said much." Lily was a quiet Métis woman. Krie felt he was trying to manage petulant children.

"Well, I think that Gladys' idea about bannock is the ticket. I mean, the craft thing is good, but not all of us make crafts. How about a bannock and craft sale?"

"We can all get behind that. If we don't do crafts or bannock, we can do set up or take the money."

The sole Haudenosaunee, Ellie, had been quietly watching Krie the entire meeting. She spoke eyes down, old school. When the meeting took a break, she approached Krie, who was making fresh tea.

"I know who you are." She looked at him frankly.

God, not this again.

"Oh?"

"You fight the 'others.' One time you got rid of a Bonewalker. I see it in your face." Krie could not breathe or speak. Finally, he changed the subject.

"Ellie, I wasn't listening, and I don't know what the heck the Council decided. What's this about fundraising with maple syrup?"

Ellie explained as if he were a child. He was alright with that; his mind was still in a whirl.

"All the Nations in what are now Quebec and Ontario harvested their maple syrup in the spring. When our land was taken, our rights to the syrup, a big trade item for us, were taken, too. Now it's a multi-million-dollar industry. Don't look shocked, it is! There's a central warehouse where syrup is stored in barrels while the ones in control wait for buyers. So, we aren't paid for the syrup until the price is high enough for the Cartel, and then they sell and pay us. It's still our syrup, in other words. For us, it's the money we need to run programs. We take our syrup, back into Native hands, then the Nations will get the insurance money, the Cartel loses nothing, and we will have our answer to our lack of funds. We'll have enough to take care of everything for a long, long time. We could make sure none of us is homeless. Everyone has enough food. The Nation gave permission to Mohawk Bill to go ahead. They're fed up waiting, too. They're good with it. They even offered to help re-steal the stuff."

Krie sat in stunned silence. What the heck had he gotten himself in for?

"We aren't common criminals." Sadie Billy was outraged as only a James Bay Cree could be. She gripped her Bible and shook her head.

"Think about this," her husband Jack was pleading with her. "We are like Robin Hood, taking something back that is ours to feed the poor. It isn't stealing when it's yours."

She was shaking her head, a stubborn look on her face.

"We have to, just for once, take back what is ours," said Ned. He was red in the face and had tears in his eyes.

"We have lost so so much. Culture. Language. Children. Our way of life. This is our chance to fight. We have to do this."

"Is that the consensus?" Krie asked. Every head in the room nodded.

"Who is going to plan this little caper?" Krie was afraid he already knew the answer.

"You're the Elders' Coordinator," Gladys said with exuberance.

Krie sighed. How the blazes was he going to pull this off?

Bill approached him after the meeting. Everyone was still talking animatedly, and he could hardly hear him above the excited voices.

"It's alright, sonny. There's eight of us who served in the military. We know how to plan a raid."

"I don't know if that's a comfort to me or not," Krie was shaking his head slowly. Bill threw his head back and laughed.

"That doesn't give me much comfort." Krie was dead serious. How in hell did he get roped into this?"

Sequoia was in the lobby when he arrived Monday morning, she was talking to the receptionist. His breath quickened. He hefted the heavy box he was carrying and nodded toward both of them, but avoided her eyes, and walked past quickly. He busied himself in the Elders' Lounge, making coffee and tea. He didn't feel anyone come up behind him.

There was never time in a day to resolve things with Sequoia. Krie was busy. Gladys packed, Krie hauled, and finally, the last load of the kid's stuff was in the van ready for the move to Mme. Brodeur's house.

"Well, that's that. The social worker has done the home visit, the paperwork is in, now we gotta get this all set up. Are you ready for this?"

The next few days were a kid tornado. Mme. Brodeur was willing to cook, but there was still the grocery shopping, laundry, cleaning, tidying, organizing appointments, and setting up daycare. Gladys was great with the children, settling them in by making everything a game. They seemed to adjust easily enough, but the house was always upside down, and Krie was going from early morning to late at night.

Krie had just arrived in the office. He switched on the light and began running through his morning ritual in preparation for the Elders. He was in the midst of arranging the coffee when a middle-aged woman appeared in the doorway. Her voice startled him.

"You're Krie, aren't you? I'm Ida. Gladys is my Mom. She told me what you did for my kids. I'm not allowed to have them back until get a job."

"Hi, Ida. The kids are fine. They think this is like camping in someone else's house."

Krie was trying to wrap his mind around everything. He was in over his head – the proposed heist, Sequoia, the kids, Gladys, what more could he get tangled up in? He walked in Mme. Brodeur's front door and was ambushed by three little bodies. Laughing, he tossed each up in the air, planted kisses and hugs, and greeted his landlady. She handed him a letter.

"Krie, can we play puppets?" Lena looked adorable pleading with her big eyes and pursed lips. She was only three but knew how to work him already.

"Sweetie, let me read this letter, it's from home, okay? Then we'll eat dinner. We can play puppets after that, k?" Lena giggled and ran to the others.

He loved these kids, the kid noise, the kid smells of peanut butter and plasticine, and even the kid mess. It brought life and happiness.

Dear Krie

Uncle says don't worry about the misunderstanding with Sequoia. He says if it is meant to be there is nothing you can do to stop it. He was laughing when he said it, but you know it's true.

Things are good here. I'm keeping an eye on Uncle. He's still slowing down but is determined to moose hunt in the next few weeks and to trap this winter. Can't keep a good man down, right?

I did put an offering out for your Grandmother and Gramma Maisey for you.

It's an early fall this year. It might only be the end of August, but it's already cold, the leaves are changed, and we had flurries yesterday.

We miss you. We were surprised that you took on somebody else's kids, but we think you did a good thing. Kids are a lot of work, but they bring happiness, and they are about the only thing a person can count on for that.

Billy and Ronnie are doing well and keep asking when you are coming back. They miss you and always want to know how come we can't visit. Billy started school (can you believe it?) I still take Ronnie everywhere, though so he can learn bush skills before he starts school next year. He is lucky to still have Uncle to learn from. He has him shooting already, at least with the .22 which he can handle. He's a strong little guy, just like his brother. Darlene went to treatment and is back in Tagish at the house. The boys visit on weekends. She seems to be doing alright. I hope that keeps up. I'm trying to work things out with her for the boys. We'll see.

That other story you told about the syrup? Those Elders are pretty badass. I think it is going to bring them to life, so just do it. I think they chose you because they trust you. Go ahead and help them out. It is a good thing to do, even though means stealing something back. To me that isn't stealing, it's just making things right. Life is never really black and white, and this is a great opportunity. You can't be too good of a guy, women like bad asses, look at me ha ha.

Not much more to say–oh Albert and Ben say hello. They are thinking about coming down to visit, but who knows if it's just talk. Thought I'd warn you ha ha.

Uncle just walked in and sends his love. The boys did the drawings for you to hang on your wall, so you won't miss them too much. You may never sleep if they are in your room ha ha. (Krie pulled out the drawings and smoothed them. He smiled at Haywire's comment – they were pretty colourful alright. One was of the boys, himself, Angus, and their dad. The other was Little Annie Lake, with the cabin, cache and outhouse. Now his gut ached with homesickness.)

Write again and tell us about Sequoia. We are waiting to hear what happens, and hope you get things straight. Nothing wrong with working hard for a good woman. It will be worth it. You are still young. Plenty of time for you to settle down. Meantime enjoy as much as you can, because we will be working you hard when you get home.

Uncle sends his love, and Lorna says send maple syrup home for the next family Potlatch. She says it would be the best giveaway ever. Send it up Greyhound, I'll go and get it and store it in Gramma's house. We're still staying down at the lake. She's with us. It's too hard for her now to live alone.

Love, Haywire, Billy, Ronnie, and Uncle Angus.

The Elders' Council was meeting again. There'd been a number of "emergency meetings." The Executive Director swung by to welcome them and to say how happy she was that they were being so active under the new Coordinator. Krie looked down, his lips twitching, and when he looked up he was ringed with innocent smiles and nods.

The Council had decided on a craft sale and bannock sale. In addition, several of them were bragging about gambling prowess, and how they had figured out a system. Gladys was the instigator and had all the staff convinced.

"This is to have a cover story for the syrup cash."

Krie was making regular trips with the Council to the Casino de Montréal. It was an impressive building that looked like a fully lit cruise ship on land. Krie found it overwhelming. The noise, hype lights, music was all a recipe for Norther homesickness. After the third trip, the Council had a visit from the Executive Director.

"Hello, Honored Elders, (rolling eyes), I am Ms. Linklater, the Executive Director of the Native Friendship Centre of Montreal."

"She thinks we're senile and don't know where we are!" Gladys whispered a bit too loudly.

"Um-Ah, While I am gratified to see you all so active of late, I can't approve the cost of your Elders' van trips to casinos.

Now, if you choose to undertake this activity, please take advantage of the casino shuttle. I have no doubt that it would be a simple matter and that Krie would be happy to facilitate it for you.

"Well, I am sure you want to get back to your meeting, I will just get back to my duties then."

"She's pretty alright, but what an apple!" Gladys looked disgusted.

"Apple?" Krie was confused.

"Yeah, red on the outside, and white on the inside. She ought to get out of those suits and into some rez mud.

"Okay, let's get down to the plan, people, please." Bill was firm.

"How does one arrange to steal barrels of syrup from a secure facility? How does one then transport it, and where? And then how does one market said syrup?" Bill was drawing on a whiteboard as if he were planning a military operation. In fact, he was.

"I have a way to steal the syrup." A circle of grey and white heads turned her way.

"S-I-P-H-O-N H-O-S-E!" Jack nodded, satisfied.

"And what do we siphon the syrup into?" Bill challenged, as if he were talking to a high school class.

"Our own barrels," Ned piped in.

"Right, now how do we get all those barrels in and out of a secured facility?"

Everyone was silent. Sadie Billy shocked them all.

"With the Elder's van." The room erupted into laughter.

"No, just listen." She was defensive.

"If we take the seats out, we can take a load, one at a time, at night." Bill was all business.

"That would mean a lot of trips – Sadie, you are the recon girl. Find out the circumference and weight of a full barrel. Measure the van and see how many barrels we can get in there. Consult the motor vehicle manual to see how much weight it can handle."

"That doesn't help us figure out how to get *in* to the secured facility," said Gladys.

There was a voice from behind the couch.

"I have a way." Everyone froze.

Krie felt sick. Who was there that had heard ever word they had said? George's head poked up. A big, smiling Inuk head of black hair. "I know how."

"How do we know you can be trusted?"

"Because I need money to get home for good, that's why. Furthermore," he said, drawing himself up and tidying his wrinkled clothes. "Like I said, I know how to get in that warehouse."

◎◎◎

The bannock sale had morphed into a Bannock Taco sale, during one of the busiest evening gatherings at the Centre. Wednesday nights were legal clinic, beading, drumming, stone carving. The Elders' kitchen was an assembly line of different kinds of bannock.

"What is this gluten-free flour?" Gladys asked Krie.

"Oh, some people believe regular flour is bad for them, so gluten-free is popular."

"I can't believe anyone would make bannock out of this stuff. It's like pancakes; it won't hold shape." She sounded frustrated.

"It's okay. It will be covered in taco stuff and nobody will notice."

"I hope not. An Indian woman takes pride in her bannock, and this is making me recon more like ashamed!"

"It will be fantastic, just put love into it." Gladys snorted at Krie who was grinning at her.

"How do you put love into something so ugly?" Ellie cackled, as she fried her large, golden and crispy bannock.

"Gladys, just make sure you get some of my beautiful frybread."

"More bread. This stuff is selling like you wouldn't believe!" Bill was on his heels.

"We have already made $350, and the glue-free is a hot seller!"

"That's not bannock, it's frybread," Ellie gently chided.

"What in blazes is the difference?"

An animated discussion broke out regarding the difference, while Krie belly laughed. Ellie and Gladys glared at him until he recovered.

"Frybread, bannock. I had no idea this was such a hot topic!"

"Frybread is a yeast dough, and bannock is a baking powder dough." Gladys was anything but patient.

"Whatever it is, keep on cooking. The Natives of Montreal want their bannock, frybread, their gluten-free, and their dairy-free, and most certainly their glue-free. And they want it now!"

An hour or so later, Bill announced the take.

"We made $857 dollars"! There was applause and grinning all around.

"Let's eat!"

"What do you say we take this money to the casino and see if we can double it?" Gladys looked gleeful.

"I don't know ... what if we lose it all?" Krie's brow was furrowed.

"Come on, sonny, live a little and have faith. I'm a card shark!" Gladys said confidently. The others nodded. Krie felt sick to his stomach.

◉◉◉

Little Charlie had been up all night screaming in pain with an earache, and Krie had not slept. His stomach was churning. Last night, the worry of the child, compounded with the enormity of the reality that he was organizing a felony and was in love with Sequoia, had kept him from sleep. In the dark of night, clarity had caused Krie to think the plan was crazy insane. Sequoia was unattainable. The responsibility for children was frightening. In the light of morning, the syrup plan seemed completely insane. He felt mildly nauseated. His head was buzzing from weakness, and he had the sense that if he stood up too quickly he would likely pass out. Coffee. That was it. He dragged himself out of the chair and got water in the coffee pot. Opening the package of coffee, half of it spilled on the counter and half on the floor.

"Hey, good news, bro. I have a probable buyer for your product." George's voice was almost in his ear. Krie jumped, spilling the coffee grounds again.

"George, you are like an Inuk Ninja!" George was grinning at him.

"Man, what's with *you*?"

"I have someone outside waiting to meet you."

"This isn't a good day."

"This is *not* a good man to keep waiting, I'll go get him."

Krie's stomach was as rough as a winter storm on Superior when he bent yet one more time to clean up the mess. He heard slow heavy steps come across the Elders' Lounge. They'd already been laughed out of a Montreal Mafia meeting, and the Hells Angels were still cackling when they had been told to get the hell out of their favorite bar. Krie turned, still squatting. He looked down at an impossibly huge pair of black Dayton work boots. His eyes slowly moved up. Huge legs in jeans, a thick waist, and the torso of a UFC heavyweight. Did this guy actually oil up? There were a lot of tattoos, obviously jail work. He reached the thick neck and the biggest head he had ever seen. The scarred Indian face wore an expression between Wes Studi as a really mean guy and one of those huge Mexican character actors who you just knew was going to shoot somebody. They stared at each other. Krie was at a loss for words.

What the hell was George thinking?

This guy looked like he was the biggest, meanest guy in the penitentiary cafeteria. This was not good, not good at all. Krie was at a loss for words. He just stared, trying to figure out how he was going to get out of this. The man stared right back. He wasn't challenging or sizing Krie up, just looking at him like a grizzly would look at you in the wild if you were face to face.

"I know who you are," the man said quietly. "You have to be Dale Post's boy."

Krie stopped breathing.

"That's the rumour," he croaked out.

"You're the spitting image of that pretty Hollywood Indian."

Krie looked at him, head tilted.

"Pretty Hollywood Indian?"

"Yeah, the boy was way too pretty for his own good. Got him in a load of trouble." The man grinned and extended a huge paw. He looked only slightly less scary when smiling with his grizzly eyes. Krie rose, swaying with the dizziness, and shook it.

"How did you know my Father?"

"That depends."

"What do you mean, that depends?"

"That depends on what side of the law you are on."

"The wrong side, apparently," Krie said, a little unhappily.

"Let's just say we were, ah, associates. He was working with an organization that my organization is affiliated with. The H.A."

"Sorry, H.A.?" asked Krie.

"Hells Angels. They're still laughing by the way." Now Krie's stomach was like a rock, and his breathing quickened. Was he now turning into his father? This wasn't how his year of discovery was supposed to go?

"Uh, coffee?" Krie asked, uncertainly.

"Sounds good – make it weak, though. I have a stomach thing."

"You're alright. I'm Danny Delorme, street name is Crazy Dan."

"So, if I am looking for you that's your street name, right?"

"Nope, but since you are a relative, you get the pleasure of knowing my real name."

"When you are ready, we can talk about Dale Post. I think it would help you to understand yourself."

"I'm not sure I am ready, but if I get that way, how do I find you?"

"George. He knows everybody who's anybody."

"I'm here to talk product."

"George, close the door, put the meeting sign on it."

"What do you want moved?"

Krie steeled himself. "Maple syrup."

Crazy Dan's huge grizzly head dropped back, his eyes closed, and he laughed. "I thought they were kidding"!

When Crazy could speak, he looked at Krie with a ridiculous grin.

"You're kidding me, right?"

"I wish I were."

"Maple effing syrup?" He was laughing again; George was grinning madly at him.

"I know, it sounds ridiculous, but did you know that a barrel of maple syrup is worth almost as much as a barrel of crude oil?" Crazy's head snapped towards Krie, eyes wide.

"And did you know that security at the Cartel syrup warehouse is non-existent?"

"Cartel?" Now Crazy laughed even harder. He had tears running out of the sides of his eyes, was slapping his huge baseball mitt hands on his knees.

"Look, if this isn't your game, put me on to someone who can buy what we are going to get."

"No, no … it's just … I never knew how much maple syrup was worth. I mean we run the usual products in demand on the street; the usual … but syrup?""

"Well, the one thing you can say about it, is that it's not exactly contraband."

"Oh, so you are thinking of crossing the border, then?"

"Well, not an official border necessarily."

"Who did you have in mind as a buyer?"

"I was thinking maple candy makers. Harder to trace, once it's turned into something else." Dan whistled, obviously impressed.

"Boy, you are much more like your Father than you know."

"That's what I'm afraid of! And maybe you should be too if we're related."

"Yeah, unfortunately, or fortunately for you, we are."

"How?"

"Your Father is my Dad's brother." There was a very long pause.

"You're my cousin!" Krie was short of breath. "You're the only one I have met from his family. I know little of him, *other than he is not resting in peace.*" There was a sarcastic edge to his voice.

"It's not that simple. He had a dark side, like us all."

"You don't say." Krie's voice was sardonic.

"You have to know the full story to have a feel for the deal."

"And you are going to tell it to me?"

"It would help you to know. It seems you only know the dark side of the man."

"I was conceived by the dark side of that man. He raped my Mother."

"It wasn't him, that's the thing, it was a Bonewalker."

"Bonewalker? You know about Bonewalkers?"

"Everybody in our culture knows about them. They either are a host of one, are terrified of them, or are the few that are the Bonewalker fighters.

"All of our cultures have stories about them, they're called different things. They are kind of like the ultimate boogie man. Parents scare kids with stories. The stories are true."

Krie was silent. He didn't know if this guy was telling the truth about being his cousin. He didn't know what this guy was up to. He didn't know what to say. He took the Northern approach and stayed very, very quiet.

Crazy Dan looked at his nails.

"I get the feeling you aren't ready to deal with the whole story of your Father. You have family here. This is where your Dad came after the tragedy."

"I will talk about that with you, and when I am ready, I should meet the family."

"All in good time. Let's get back to his sweet heist." His maybe cousin was chuckling quietly.

"Sweet heist, good one."

"Money is money, and it's low risk, so … a definite possibility. Let me run it by my guys, and if they won't bite, maybe the H.A. would."

"Nah, chucked us out of their bar. Do I need to come with you to negotiate?"

"Yeah. They'll want to see who is making the offer. Get your presentation down. Get your PowerPoint ready so you can give as much information as possible." He could have been a banker the way he was talking.

"PowerPoint? You're kidding, right?"

Whoever this Crazy Dan was, Krie liked him. He liked him a lot. George grinned and winked at Krie.

◎◎◎

It was casino time. Krie was so exhausted it took everything in him to find an excuse to sign the van out, get the Elders organized and in the van. George insisted on coming.

So many Elders wanted to go that Krie was going to have to make three trips. "Good," he thought. "I won't be there to see them lose the money." He handed Gladys the packet of cash from the fundraising. She grinned.

"Don't you worry, sonny. I'm gonna make us some chimichangas."

"It's money we need."

"Have some faith in old Granny, you'll see."

Krie was not all together sure he would be in his right mind by the time they needed to return. He slumped down in his seat and fell asleep. He woke when he heard a huge kafuffle. He hoisted himself up in his seat, and there was Gladys being escorted out the front door by security, with the other Elders trailing in walkers, wheelchairs, and limping along on canes. Gladys was shouting.

"Just because an old lady has some luck, you gotta throw her old bones out? It's because I'm Native, isn't it! You should be ashamed of yourselves." What now, Krie yawned and stretched, swung the bus door open, and hopped straight to the ground.

"What seems to be the issue?" he directed this to the security guards.

"We were directed to ask this lady to exit the premises. It is suspected that she has a system. She won $10,000 in 10 minutes!"

"Can't an innocent old lady have fun? Isn't that the idea of a casino? So, it's okay for you to have a system to take my money, but not okay for an innocent old lady to win?"

"Just get her out of here, get them all out of here, now."

"Krie, I want to charge this casino with harassment against Elders."

"Let's just go, Gladys, we can sort this out later."

Krie nodded to security who let Gladys go. She slapped in their direction, tidied her clothes, and gave a harrumph at them over her shoulder. They were looking back at her as they took the front stairs to the entrance.

"You won?" Krie was incredulous.

"Sure, in the heck did!" Gladys had a huge and mischievous grin, and her wrinkled eyes were sparkling.

"He's wrong though, it wasn't $10,000."

"Oh, too bad."

"It was $100,000."

"If we hit all the casinos we can get to, I can use my system, and we can make a lot of money. It'll be the cover for the cash we will make in the heist. We can say I won it at bingo."

"Gladys, please tell me you don't have a gambling system."

"Yup, I used to deal way-back when I worked in the Indian Casinos in the States. Dealing cards was a bore. Until a shark came in. I watched him. I figured out his deal. I'm gonna take this to my grave, but I know how to win, and win big."

"You got thrown out. You want to get thrown out of every casino we go to?"

"No, I needed to win big and fast tonight. After this I can take my time maybe, and win once at the end of a night of losing. I know how to lose, too, you know."

"We can talk about all this later. Let's drop off all these folks, and we can all recon at the Centre tomorrow."

When Krie pulled up at the Friendship Centre, the lights were still on. Krie had lost all track of time and heaved a sigh of relief. He helped the Elders off the van, and said,

"Let's have a quick meeting." The Elders were as excited as Krie had ever seen them. In the Elders' Lounge, George was making tea and coffee. The chattering was so loud it sounded like a drinking party. Krie had never seen the Elders so riled up. George had to raise his voice to Krie.

"Okay, everyone," Krie tried to bring them to order.

"EVERYONE!" Krie stopped them from speaking.

"Sorry I had to raise my voice, but you guys are like a pack of geese." There were giggles, and Gladys looked offended.

"The story is, I won at bingo; the end." Gladys said.

"What do you all think, is that the story?"

"We have to find other casinos. They aren't going to let us back into the one we just got chucked from." Gladys had obviously thought this through.

"Time to hit the big time. Time for the Akwesasne Mohawk Casino Resort." The group's reaction was like kids near Christmastime, when hope makes anything possible.

"Uh, where is it?" Sweat was breaking out on Krie's upper lip.

"It's in Mohawk territory alright," Ned was smiling at Krie.

"Our traditional territory was big – in Upstate New York."

Krie knew for a fact that he was not a good liar. How the hell was he going to pull this off?

Gladys stomped her walker into Krie's office, where he was busily mapping out the logistics for the casino trip to New York.

"I want you to meet my friend Mavis."

Behind her, was a tall, dignified older woman, with long, white hair in braids. She was slightly bent in the back and deeply striking. Something about her took Krie's breath away. He quickly stood and held out a chair for her. She sat. He drew closer and as he approached to shake her hand, he found himself looking into the wisest eyes he had ever seen. It was like looking into the eyes of a wolf. His heart quickened. Her brown face was lined with a lifetime of smiling.

"I'm Krie." He held out his hand.

"Hello, Krie. You certainly are everything Gladys described." Her voice was like the wind in the Northern trees. Like water in a creek, flowing through his beloved meadows. He was struck dumb. He felt as though he were in the presence of both Sopiah and Gramma Maisey. His eyes filled with tears.

"I'm Mavis Mankiller."

"She isn't well." said Gladys. "I figured that she is too good to cross over without a little corrupting. We all need a little balance in life." Mavis' voice was calming, mesmerizing.

"I just want to see the beauty of our relatives all over Turtle Island. I want to see that our people are doing well. I want to see how our people are rising up. And I want to win some money for my family back home, before I die. I want them to have good houses, I want them to have money to educate their children, and I want to pay for the reserve to have good drinking water. They have been on a boil water advisory for *30 years*."

"Gramma, we will make that happen." Krie felt as though he wanted to lay his life down for this promise, for this beautiful and gentle-spirited soul.

"Thank you, sonny. It may seem like an odd wish for a traditional woman, but one must do what one must do."

"There is such a thing where there is good intent."

"I know, Gramma, that's why I'm letting these bandits lead me astray."

All three of them laughed. Gladys looked like she had already won another jackpot, and Mavis and Krie went out to make them all some tea.

Krie walked into the Executive Director's office. He had his stories straight and was deep breathing. Kristine was on the phone. She motioned for him to sit. As he waited, he breathed slowly, in and out, in and out, in and out. He focused on the medicine gifts that littered her office. He could sense that she had no attachment to the medicines by the way they were displayed with impressive Inuit carvings, Navajo pottery, and the like.

"So, Krie, what can I do for you?"

"Well, the Elders, as you know, had some bingo luck, at Akwesasne in New York.

There was a voice from the door. "Krie, may I speak to you privately?"

It was Sequoia. Krie's heart quickened, as he saw her high-colour and the dark seriousness in her eyes. He nodded and when he reached the door, she said quietly, "Come into my office." This was it.

She wanted to talk. Finally. Relief flooded him, while he felt the muscle in his jaw tense; this was not the best time. She closed the door and motioned for him to sit down.

"Sorry, Sequoia, I don't have much time. We are on a tight schedule for the trip; the itinerary, you know," he flushed, feeling like an idiot.

"Krie, I want you to be very, very careful. You're going to run into a Bonewalker."

Krie felt numb, and his blood was singing an old song he did not want to hear. He couldn't move.

"How ... ?"

"Dreams. I get warnings in dreams. I saw you fighting one. Krie, this one is very old and very cunning. Please be on your guard." Her eyes were full of concern and were brimming with tears. Her bottom lip trembled.

"I don't want anything to happen to you, Krie."

"Sequoia you and I – we need to talk."

"I know, Krie, and you have to leave." His head was swimming.

"Sequoia, I don't know how to begin to sort out what has happened between us."

"That's okay, because I do. I am an idiot. I am truly sorry. I was told in no uncertain terms by my Grandmother how foolish I have been not to trust you and tell you everything. She told me everything. Krie, you're a good man, and we can talk when you get back, but for now, take this with you." She crossed to him and kissed him slowly and gently on the cheek. He shivered, and her heat shot through his body like electricity.

He reached out, gently took her hand and kissed the palm, closed it, and smiled.

"Keep this, until I see you." The tears that filled her eyes flowed down her cheeks as she smiled at him. "And I married McNevin ONLY so he could get into the country. We were never a thing."

Krie's heart was as light as eagle down on a Northern lake. Maybe, just maybe, everything was going to be alright.

When they pulled up to the casino, Gladys chortled, "Hey, just for fun, ask for parking service." Everyone laughed.

Krie pulled the van up to the complex.

"Okay, have at 'er. I will go and check us all in."

He grinned and shook his head as they piled out, and limped, rolled, and walked in the front doors.

Krie was grateful for the busboy, who loaded all the bags on carts, and showed him to the rooms. He washed his face and headed to the elevator. He was permatired. He rubbed his face with his hands and that is when he caught the smell of rotting evil. His head jerked up. Bonewalker!

Krie was on edge as he walked into the casino. All the Elders were gambling.

"Okay, hit me, Granddaughter!" The dealer snapped out a card.

"Twenty-one," she announced flatly. The old girls cheered wildly. Krie was exhausted by midnight when Gladys' winnings reached over $300,000. Security had arrived when she hit $75,000. She threw in a few losses. They could do nothing. Gladys winked and waved at the security camera above her head.

"Don't worry, I'm quitting while I'm ahead," she shouted.

Krie was relieved when she cashed-out and had the desk put her winnings in the hotel safe. All he wanted was to lay down and sleep.

He had just drifted off when the phone rang. Confused for a moment, he did not recognize his surroundings.

"Hello?"

"Krie, it's Sequoia." He sat up.

"What is it?"

"The kids, Krie, they woke up screaming just now. They all smelled something rotten, and they were all terrified. Krie, it's here."

◉◎◎

The trip home could not go fast enough. Only Gladys knew about the call, and she and Krie had been up late, praying. They had called Sequoia back at 4:30 a.m. and all had been quiet. Krie had a sick feeling and was worried for Sequoia and the three babies. He knew Gladys was as well; she hardly spoke on the trip back and looked grim. He knew neither of them had slept much. He did not want to have to take on another Bonewalker but when it came to innocent children, there was no way he was not going to go to battle. He was dizzy with exhaustion when he and Gladys finally pulled up to Mme. Brodeur's house.

Sequoia was pale, and the kids were as excited and noisy as ever to see both him and their Grandmother. Mme. Brodeur had lunch ready.

"So? How was the trip?"

201

"Three hundred big ones," Gladys announced.

"Wonderful"! Mme. Brodeur clapped her hands together and put lunch on the table.

"Krie, we have to plan; we have to secure the room up there."

"I know. I don't know why I didn't think of it before." His head was down.

The three of them walked with the abalone shell full of smoking medicines and prayed. Krie put the protection medicine he had been given from the North on the windowsills, and above the door.

"I think we had better do the entire house." Sequoia was serious.

"Yes, I think you are absolutely right," Krie said quietly, as he picked up a stench in the corner.

There on the floor was a rotting piece of meat. Tinged with green and covered with maggots.

"I am not leaving here, Krie. I am staying until we send this Bonewalker out of this world."

"Sequoia, I am worried enough about everyone here, I don't want to have to worry about you as well."

She reached out her hand and touched his.

"Krie, I can help you fight, and I am staying."

As dusk crept forward to steal the light, Krie, Gladys, and Sequoia shared tea in the kitchen. Mme. Brodeur was busy with laundry in the basement.

"The basement!" The three exchanged horrified glances. They had forgotten the basement! As they walked down the stairs to the basement, Mme. Brodeur looked up, questioningly. They smudged every corner, and Krie carefully placed protection medicine at each window and the door to the outside.

Gladys took the first watch. Krie knew that between 2 and 4 was the greatest time of danger. At 1 o'clock, he sent Gladys to bed. She hugged him tight and looked into his eyes before she clumped into her room behind her walker. Krie sat, in a circle of tobacco, in the living room. At a few minutes to 2, Sequoia appeared in the doorway. She wore a long, yellow ceremonial dress with black, white, and red ribbons, and his heart quickened as she crossed to him. His breathing was shallow and quick.

"Krie, I am going to stay with you here until morning. Gladys doesn't need to know that you and I don't have separate watches. We can do this together." He sighed. He did not want to say yes, but something told him to agree. He nodded. They held hands as they sat, waiting in the night silence.

When the stench reached them, they both stiffened – jumping when they heard a blood-curdling howl from right outside the window and the scratching at the side of the house.

Krie felt chills go from his scalp to his feet. Sequoia shot a look at him and began to sing. The howling grew louder as the stench grew stronger. They both coughed and retched. Sequoia held his hand tighter and sang louder. Krie did not know the song, so he prayed. He called on Uncle, Grandmother, Gramma Maisey. He re-lit the smudge.

When they heard the scratching coming from the basement door in the kitchen, they looked at each other in horror. Sequoia sang louder, and Krie prayed harder. The door rattled, and Krie rose. Sequoia pleaded with her eyes and grasped his arm. He shot her a determined glance, grasped the tobacco, and tiptoed to the basement door. There was silence, then a loud awful howl just on the other side.

The stench was so overwhelming, Krie threw up. He heard cackling, as he placed a solid straight line of Northern medicine in front of the door. He felt Sequoia behind him. She bent with her hand over her mouth and emptied the contents of her stomach. They stood together, and she sang louder, as he prayed harder. The rattling and scratching stopped, and the pong slowly abated. It was gone. They looked at each other.

"Let's clean this up." They did so in silence. When they were finished, they both smelled the coffee. They turned with tired eyes to the aroma, and Mme. Brodeur placed three cups on the table.

"After a battle such as that, you deserve some strong coffee," she said in perfect English. Sequoia and Krie smiled tiredly at one another. It was then that Mme. Brodeur swung round with urgency in her voice.

"The wood door. You forgot the small door where we bring wood for the old stove into the basement. It's behind the grey blanket to keep the cold out." Krie and Sequoia glanced at each other, then at Mme. Brodeur.

"I know from my young years what *that* was. I knew who you two were when I first set eyes on you. I knew why you were smudging the house. I know, too, that you will drive away that beast. But go now, Krie, and put that medicine at the wood door. Hurry!"

When Gladys rose the next morning, she was horrified to learn that they had let her sleep.

"I can't believe you tried to fight that thing by yourselves!" she scolded.

"Well, they drove it away." Mme. Brodeur beamed at the two young people.

"Well, wake me up the next time it comes back. I'll get it the hell away from here!"

"What are you going to do? Challenge it to a game of blackjack?" Krie teased.

"No, beat it senseless with my walker!" All four of them laughed until tears ran down their cheeks.

"It won't attack here next time, but we need to make little protection bundles for the children." Krie was serious. They all looked at one another, frozen. The children.

◉◉◉

Nobody had thought to check on them with Mme. Brodeur's room next to theirs. There was complete silence upstairs. Krie was holding his breath when he opened their door. They were gone! Vanished. Seemingly into the air.

Krie felt as though he had been punched in the gut. He felt the blood drain out of his legs and his head buzzed with the terror that swam through his tangled thoughts. He frantically searched every room on the top floor. There was no sign of them. Then he saw the window as he passed by their bedroom door. It was open. Tears ran out of his eyes with shame and horror. How could he have not put a complete circle of protection around them? How could he have not ensured that someone stayed in the room with them? He was distraught as he walked back into the kitchen. The three women looked up to see him in the doorway, white-faced, almost panting.

"Oh my God." Gladys's hand went to her throat.

"Krie, what is it?"

"Mon Dieu!"

His reply came out in a sob.

"They're gone. The children are gone." He dropped into a chair, put his head on his arms and sobbed.

"Police, we must call the police."

"And explain this how?"

"Just say they were abducted, when we were sleeping."

"Oh my God, how could I have let this happen?"

"Krie, none of us thought they were in danger if we were trying to prevent the Bonewalker from getting in. We checked on them only an hour ago."

"It got in. I don't know how." Krie was still crying. His own abduction played in his mind's eye like a video. He stood, tall and with a dark look on his face, which was still covered in tears.

"I will find them. If it is the last thing I do, I will find them. Gladys, I am so sorry." She nodded miserably.

"What are you going to do?"

"I'm going to pray, and I am going to ask to see where they are. Then I am going to go, and I am going to get them back. And nothing will ever harm them again. If anything bad has happened to them, I will never forgive myself!"

It was then they heard the little thump from upstairs. Krie and Sequoia flew up the staircase, and Gladys pulled herself up one step at a time. Mme. Brodeur sat at the table, crossing herself, eyes closed tight. Something made Krie open the old closet door in their bedroom. They were sleeping in tangles of blankets, all curled around each other on the floor. Krie took a deep breath, and a moan of relief escaped him. One of the children stirred, yawned, and looked up.

"Hi, Uncle Krie. We heard Madam get up to make breakfast so we decided to play hide-from-the-monster until it was ready. This was the best spot we found. He couldn't even see us from the window if he tried like last night. Where did you hide?

The child's innocent smile almost broke Krie's heart in two.

He and Sequoia lifted the younger ones carefully into the bed and covered them.

"Come downstairs, Josh. I am going to make you the biggest pancakes you have ever seen!" Josh's sleepy face broke into a wide smile. He reached for Krie's hand, and he padded in little bear feet down the stairs. Krie thought it was the most precious sound he had ever heard.

"There *was* a monster at the window, but he couldn't get in. I could tell. He was trying to scare us. I was brave, but Lena and Charlie were scared of him. We curled up like squirrels under the covers, and then he went away."

"How did you know that he went away?"

"Because he didn't scratch on the window no more, and we heard you singing downstairs. We knew he did not like the song. I was really brave. I like the song. It made me sleepy. I was going to tell you about it, but I fell asleep."

Krie and Sequoia whispered on the back porch.

"Last night wasn't even the First Round."

"I know, Krie. I don't really know what to think about that."

"I think he was trying to get our attention by scaring the kids."

"I think you're right. I'm not leaving. You're not going to do this alone."

Krie smiled and tilted his head.

"I can't lie, I would like that. But I have a feeling the Bonewalker is not going to attack here next. I don't like the thought of you being alone at your place. He may attack you there. He'll know that you mean the world to me." She smiled, and her eyes were soft. Then her brow furrowed.

"What do you think he is going to do?"

"I don't know. But there's no way for him to get in here. He can't cross that medicine. So, he'll try somewhere else. And I don't know how he will attack for the first round."

"I can't help but be afraid." She leaned into him.

"Sequoia, I'm terrified. I've only fought one Bonewalker, and he almost killed me. What if I take one look in his eyes, and I can't defeat him?"

"Krie, you *have* to. I can't lose you!"

◉◉◉

Krie rose in the morning, hardly having slept. His mind was clear despite his aching body. Something had bothered him all night long; kept waking him up. Each time he found himself sitting upright, with a sense of apprehension. It was puzzling, and his thoughts went over the sequence of the events the night before. Something was wrong, but he did not know what. Over and over the night before played like a video as he tried to find the one clue – he needed to answer this sense of dread in his gut. He heard the children come down the stairs. He hugged each of them as they got to the bottom step where he stood and whispered for them to be quiet.

"Sequoia and Gramma are probably going to sleep late; let's play a game in the basement so that we don't wake them, okay?"

"I not like the basement."

"I know, it's just for a couple of hours, though, okay?"

Krie lugged baskets of plastic building bricks down the basement stairs, the kids tumbling like puppies after him.

"We are going to build a city, okay?" They all knelt on the carpet that he had put down for them.

"Otay." The youngest was looking up at him, with his crooked smile.

Krie reached over and planted a kiss on his nose. Charlie giggled. They loved to build.

When they were engrossed in the project, he went up the stairs for coffee. On the second step, his hair rose all over his body. He stopped, listened, and there was nothing. He shook his head at himself and continued up the stairs. He glanced back when Charlie let out a squeal. He smiled as he walked into the kitchen, got his coffee, and sank heavily into a chair.

He allowed his muscles to relax and stretched his lanky body out.

Mme. Brodeur came from the pantry with jars of canning in a box.

"These are cool, must put them in the basement to store."
He nodded as she made her way down the stairs. He heard her
stop halfway down. There was silence, so he sipped his coffee,
and pondered what the feeling of dread was that he could not
shake. He left the table and as quietly as possible and went
upstairs.

Standing outside Sequoia's door, he could hear her breathing. He let out his breath and went to Gladys' door. When he
could hear her snoring, he went back down to the kitchen.
Everyone was fine. What was this feeling that would not leave
him? He shook it off and turned the radio on in the kitchen,
leaving the volume low.

Mme. Brodeur smiled at the children from where she was
carefully placing her neatly labelled canning jars on a nearby
shelf. Beams of sunlight fell on their tousled heads while
they talked in childlike tones about their city. As she put her
foot on the bottom step, she was struck with anxiety. She
paused. This had not happened in a long time. She scanned
the basement, looking for a cause. There was nothing but
the three darlings on the carpet, happily playing. She shook
her head and walked up the stairs to the kitchen. At the top,
she shivered as a cold crept across her skin. She saw Krie at the
table.

"Coffee. That will shake it."

"Shake what?"

"I don't know, a bad feeling."

"I think we are all feeling it, it's the dread, the waiting. It's
almost the worst of it – the wait."

"Perhaps." She crossed to the stove and poured a cup of
coffee.

"But did you think that perhaps we have forgotten something, or perhaps made some mistake?"

"I can't think what. I have been going over it all, and I get this feeling, but really can't think of what is causing it."

Mme. Brodeur sat opposite Krie.

"Perhaps, maybe, we must be ready for anything."

"Yes, we should be." Krie's expression was grim.

Sequoia was in deep peaceful sleep. She was visiting her Great Grandmother. They were having tea in an old wall tent. Great Grandmother had boiled water on top of the little wood stove in the tent and had made tea in the chipped pot Sequoia had always loved. She poured steaming tea into enamel camp mugs. They sat together and did not speak. Sequoia felt peaceful, happy.

"The man the Old Ones have chosen for you, he is a good man," Great Grandmother said in her slow way.

"Your lives will not be simple. You will always have to help people. But it will be good. You will always have what you need. It is good that you are fighting together."

Sequoia nodded. She felt the love for Krie in her chest, warm and swelling so that it caused tears to fill her eyes.

"I love him, Great Grandmother, and I know he loves me. We may have been chosen for one another, but there is true love between us." Great Grandmother nodded and smiled.

"Granddaughter, that was the way of it in the old times, with the chosen marriages."

"Are we going to defeat this Bonewalker?"

"It is not for me to say. Something has been forgotten."

"What? What is it that we have forgotten?"

"To trap it outside."

"I don't understand, Great Grandmother."

There was another voice from the door. It was Great Grandfather, peering in, his long braid over his shoulder.

"Always make …"

"Krie, Krie!" There was a pounding up the stairs. He knocked at her door.

"Come in, Krie, for God's sake, just come in!" He heard the fear in her voice.

"What is it, Sequoia?"

"A dream – I was told not to trap a Bonewalker inside. Oh my God, Krie!" She burst into tears. He stepped to the bed, sat and held her gently. She threw him off.

"Please, Krie, listen. We trapped the Bonewalker INSIDE the medicine line, not the outside!"

"Charlie wants to play hide-and-seek." Josh looked grumpy.

"I wanna build!"

"Just one turn each, okay?" Lena cajoled.

"Awright. Charlie, you go first."

Charlie half hid behind the hot-water tank. Lena and Josh pretended not to see him and spent a few minutes loudly discussing where he could be.

Bonewalker was muttering, enraged. He was pacing under the basement stairs, with two long sticks. They tapped like giant spider legs back and forth on the cement. He was in a fury at being trapped in the basement, encircled by the medicine lines. Stealing from his hiding place, he crept toward the biggest boy. He placed an icy hand on Joshua, who froze. Josh peed himself but did not resist when the Bonewalker guided him with a clawed hand to a small closet-like room under the stairs. He could not utter a sound.

Krie stared at Sequoia in horror. Something was wrong. They were rooted to the spot. It was then they heard the scream.

Krie and Sequoia dashed to the basement,

"What is it? What's happened?"

Gladys was at the top of her stairs with her walker, a mask of fear on her face. From where she stood, she could see nothing.

Sequoia and Krie were frantically searching.

"Josh is gone!"

"He was right here one moment ago!" Mme. Brodeur was white-faced and holding one hand to her chest.

"They were playing hide-and-go-seek, and you know they aren't good at hiding, I could see all three of them right there. I turned to put this box of canned tomatoes on the shelf and was arranging them. I turned back and ... gone." Gladys' voice was harsh.

"Are any of the doors down there unlocked?"

"All locked. The locks are too high for a child."

Sequoia knelt in front of Lena and Charlie.

"What happened to Josh?"

"The man. He tooked him." Sequoia and Krie exchanged a panicked glance.

"What man, sweetie? How did the man get in here?"

"We are playing hide-and-go-seek. Yeah, 'n when I counted an' I peeked; I saw a man take Joshua!" Lena clapped her hand over her mouth, and her eyes were big.

"We need to know where they went."

"They melted."

"Melted?"

"Like *Startrek* on TV when they are going in the 'porter."

"When they say they are beaming someone up?"

"Yeah!"

Sequoia stood, facing Krie. She had tears in her eyes.

"Have you ever heard of this?"

"No, my first was in the form of a man, and came and went just like we do."

"What are we dealing with? And what do we do now?"

"I wish I knew."

⊙⊙⊙

Sequoia's Grandmother was in the living room kneeling on a star blanket, with her sacred pipe; her altar laid out. Gladys, Mme. Brodeur, Lena, Charlie, Sequoia and Krie all knelt around the blanket. As she began, Krie sang the pipe-filling song. She was deliberate in her movements and her prayer. The room was fragrant with her medicine that burned in an abalone shell. The smoke slowly curled toward the ceiling, creating a sweet haze. The fragrance was as a soothing memory of ceremonies past and calmed each and everyone in the room. The children were quiet, and watching, sensing the seriousness of the adults. Krie glanced around the circle. Gladys had her eyes closed tight, and the muscles of her face were working. Her jaw was tense. Sequoia was composed, sitting with legs to the side and her head slightly down. Mme. Brodeur sat, legs straight out in front of her and eyes fixed on the pipe. Krie inhaled and closed his eyes.

Grandmother had each one pray aloud in their own way as she held the pipe up and said her own prayer. Krie relaxed. He allowed his mind to still. He followed the rhythm of his breath, inhale, exhale, inhale, exhale. His prayers were for the safety of Joshua. A thought crept in. What if Joshua was going to suffer the same fate he had during his own abduction? He willed the thought from his mind and focused again on his breath. Inhale, exhale, inhale exhale, slow and deep. Focused and deliberate. Then, like a flash, there was the Bonewalker, and Joshua. The stairs! They were under the basement stairs!

When Grandmother finished her ceremony, she lit the pipe. The sweet aroma of tobacco filled the room. As each drew in smoke, there was a crackle from the bowl. The pipe was passed until it was done. Grandmother took it carefully, lifted it one more time, and they all prayed their gratitude. The fragrance of the pipe tobacco hung, spicy and sweet, like love, like hope. Krie opened his eyes. Everyone looked relaxed and peaceful. Grandmother spoke as she carefully put away her pipe.

"This being is different. This being is an old being and has learned many cunning ways. We must be very strong. We must have deep faith in our traditional beliefs, in our prayers. We must all be united in fighting this. The child is safe. He is unconscious. But we have little time; his missing his Mother is what allowed the Bonewalker to get to him. We must help him with this."

"Grandmother, I have seen where they are."

"Where is that?"

"We trapped the Bonewalker inside. We created a medicine line, thinking he was outside, when all the time, he was under the stairs."

"Why did we not smell him?" Sequoia had a look of horror.

"Because this one is old. They know how to mask the smell," Gladys said, in a flat voice.

"I heard a story long ago. I remembered it during the ceremony. It was about a family in my community generations ago. They dealt with a Bonewalker who could appear and disappear. The thing is the child cannot. The Bonewalker cannot hide the child once we know where he is. We must lure that horrible creature out and someone must sneak in behind him and get Joshua."

Sequoia shivered and a look of horror momentarily crossed her face. Mme. Brodeur played with the rings on her hands. Gladys looked angry – determined – a storm of emotion passing across her face. Krie was silent for a moment. He stomped a foot on the floor like a bull moose warning.

"I know what I have to do."

"You aren't alone Krie, I will fight alongside you."

"This is too dangerous; I have never done it before."

"I am going to be there." He knew Sequoia well enough already not to argue. He squeezed her shoulder.

"Is there anything you need me to prepare?"

"Just get your strongest protection medicine and put it on if you haven't already."

Each member of the household got ready. The children were strangely withdrawn and quiet. They were in the TV room, watching cartoons on TV when Krie walked in.

"Are you okay?"

"Charlie wants Josh back," said Lena, rubbing her tiny big-sister palms together. He's scared."

Charlie looked up at Krie with sombre eyes. They were the wise eyes, of a child that knows far too much, far too young. He knelt by Charlie and picked him up. Charlie wrapped his little arms around his neck, his legs around him and put his little head on Krie's shoulder. Krie's heart opened like a tiny wildflower. This little one was dependent on him. He felt like a one-man army about to fight the battle of his life. His blood surged. He was past worry, and full of the adrenaline of a man who must do the impossible with nothing but is prepared in every way for the fight of his life. It wasn't about outcome; it was about the gift of trust from this little boy.

"Kryptite," Charlie said softly.

"What?" Krie pulled back and looked into Charlie's little face.

"The bad man. Kryptite."

"We are watching Superman; Charlie knows that Kryptonite makes him sick."

"Charlie, do you know what the bad man's Kryptonite is?"

"That medatin you put all around." Krie's stomach lurched. Of course. If the medicine could trap the Bonewalker, it could also weaken him! He gave Charlie an enormous hug and kissed him on the cheek then put him gently on the carpet. He picked up Lena and held her close. He put her down, and they looked up at him with absolute trust.

"I'm going to get Joshua," he said. "I want you to ask Creator to help me. Can the two of you do that?"

They nodded, serious. Lena turned off the TV.

"Charlie, let's make an altar." Krie smiled and nodded at Gladys who sat nearby with tears in her eyes.

"You know the drill, Gladys."

"I will pray the paint off the walls." Krie grinned and nodded holding a bucket of medicine. She shot him a look of love.

"You be careful, my boy!"

"Will I do, Gladys?"

"You will do," she nodded, as a single tear slipped down her face.

Krie painted himself with the powder of medicine of the North. He painted Sequoia. He took a bucket of it and descended the stairs to the basement. Sequoia was on his heels, hand on his back. Mme. Brodeur was positioned at the top of the stairs with another bucket of medicine.

The stairs squeaked long and loud in the silence as Krie and Sequoia slowly put their weight on each. Krie could hear Sequoia's quick breaths. He stopped and turned his head.

"Take deep breaths. Get yourself in that state of quiet that you do when you pray." She nodded, mindful of the gravity of his words. They took the next step. Now they were on the cement. They turned toward the small old wooden door that led to the space under the stairs when they heard a movement. Krie could feel the blood surging through his body. Energy surged like a riptide, and he kept his breath even. He began to say his spirit name under his breath. Sequoia began to chant her own. They approached the door in silence. Krie grasped the handle, then turned.

There was nothing. Krie's heart dropped. How? Then there it was. A hole to outside, a tiny light shining through the brick.

Sequoia grasped his arm and pointed with her face half turned in horror. There was Josh wrapped in a spider cocoon in a hammock hanging tight up to the ceiling of the room. Krie took hold of him and began to pull. Sequoia prayed aloud.

Once wrestled free, Krie put him in Sequoia's arms.

"Take him and go." She did not argue. The child was unconscious. Krie plugged the opening with medicine. He lined the entire door to the little room with medicine.

He sang a song – loud, and clear, before going back up the stairs.

Grandmother had put out her altar, and the child was laying on it. The others were kneeling around him, praying silently. Krie entered the room, and painted Gladys, Mme. Brodeur, Lena and Charlie.

"Where is the Bonewalker?" Gladys finally summoned the courage to ask.

"Right there," Krie pointed the polite way, with his lower lip, to Joshua.

Mme. Brodeur wilted like a wet dishcloth and folded to the floor. Sequoia was frozen, and Gladys leaned toward the woman where she lay. They attended to her while Krie carefully prepared. He placed a medicine line all around the child. He began to paint the child with the medicine when he heard Mme. Brodeur's voice.

"I'm alright, yes, yes, I'm alright."

Grandmother began to sing, and Sequoia joined her. The old voice and the young voice wove and swooped like swallows in the air. The hair went up on Krie's body. When he painted the child's feet, Josh began to tremble. He began to shake so hard that his teeth rattled.

Sequoia's singing was full of tears; a mourning song. Still, they sang. The child began to thrash to and fro, as if he were fighting something, his arms hitting the air, his legs kicking. Gladys and Mme. Brodeur prayed aloud, and the other children began to call Joshua's name. Josh moaned and spittle dripped came from his open mouth in a long string. He was babbling unintelligibly. The songs, prayers, calls grew louder, and Josh's yells sounded now like they were underwater beneath their blanket cover. As if he were struck by lightning, Josh leapt in one motion to his feet! He spun, arms out, so fast that he began to blur. The blanket tangled his feet and he fell hard to one side. He was still. He was not breathing.

Krie heard everyone crying now, as they prayed and sang, their voices desperate. The children were calling Joshua's name in piteous kitten voices, pleading. Krie put his face over Josh's mouth. No breath. His lips were starting to turn blue.

He quickly applied medicine to the child's chest, and lips. Then he began CPR. Counting, pumping, blowing, counting, pumping, blowing. He checked. Nothing! He continued counting, pumping, blowing, counting, pumping, blowing. Nothing. Tears coursed down his face. He would not give up. He stopped and roared up, "*Manitou, Neechiewagan!*" He began again. The women were sobbing their song, and the others their prayers. It raised the hair on the whole of Krie's body. Sweat poured off him, and dripped onto the child's face, making water drops on the black of the medicine. Still, he worked, gritting his teeth, counting, pumping, blowing. He called the child's name with the other children, loudly.

"Joshua!" Krie's mind was swimming, his heart ached as though it was feeling every hurt he had ever known. His body trembled with the exertion of a spirit on fire. Just when he thought he could do no more, the child stirred and sat up. He smiled at everyone.

"I'm hungry." There was an explosion of tearful laughter and tears of happiness. Grandmother was firm as she motioned Gladys and Sequoia back when they reached out to the child to hold him.

She took out her pipe and loaded it.

"This time, it's a ceremony for gratitude."

His shirt and pants were soaked with sweat. He ran his shirt sleeve across his face, blinking burning sweat out of his eyes. When he placed the medicine into the furnace, on the coals, there was a loud and terrible hissing. He stayed until it was all consumed.

They all smoked the pipe in silence. When no more smoke rose from the bowl, Grandmother carefully clean-smudged each piece, and placed them back into her pipe bag. Krie was spent; still vibrating with exhaustion and effort. The weakness left him with a sound ringing in his ears and a feeling of buzzing nausea in his stomach.

Grandmother held her pipe bag out to Krie in both hands. He was confused. Sequoia began weeping as if her heart would break. Krie's heart had not slowed, and now it felt as though it was pounding like a big drum. Gladys motioned to him to take it. He did as he was told, reaching out for it with both hands.

She motioned back and forth three more times. On the fourth pass Krie accepted the pipe.

"You have saved the life of this child. You have banished that creature. This pipe I pass to you now: Treat it like a child. Always respect the teachings that come with it. The pipe will teach you."

Tears flowed down Krie's face. He held the pipe in his arms as though it was a baby. He nodded to Grandmother, who smiled at him tenderly. He was overcome with emotions. The relief that the child was safe gave him pride and satisfaction at having banished the Bonewalker. There was a new feeling like he was a child again. The pipe was a whole new life. He now understood why Sequoia was weeping. Grandmother spoke.

"We must feed the old ones and your new baby." Krie knew she was referring to the pipe. "Krie, stay behind for a while. I will teach you how to care for your new child. And we must prepare a feast!"

They all got busy in the kitchen together. The atmosphere was happy, and light. Mme. put the radio on, and the room was filled with the happy simple music of the '50s. The children danced while standing on chairs, while others stood at the counter peeling carrots and potatoes. Grandmother was preparing frybread. Mme. Brodeur was mixing a cake. Sequoia and Krie were preparing deer stew. The children helped to put out the spirit plate. Grandmother had Krie put the tobacco down and say the gratitude prayer.

"Uncle Angus, please enjoy this food. Grandmother shares it with him and knows that I love and miss you all terribly. Gramma Maisey, I hope you like this different kind of frybread. Thank you all for your help. Thank you to all the warriors and Medicine Carriers of old that I have called upon for help. Thank you from the bottom of each of our hearts!" They stood holding hands in the circle and holding silence, for a long time. They did not see the man outside peering at them from behind a tree.

It wasn't until they all let go of one another's hands and embraced that they heard the voice.

"Hey, do I smell frybread?" They turned, and Krie laughed when he spied George. All he could see in the dark was his smile.

"You know, George, most people just knock on the door!"

"Well, igloos don't have doors, so ..." Everyone laughed.

Grandmother said,

"So, it was *you* that was helping us." George's permasmile was replaced by a rare serious expression.

"I felt it so strongly. That you all needed my help. That something was really wrong. One of you was in big trouble. I was taught long ago never to ignore those Spidey senses. I felt something in the basement. I stood outside the house where there seemed to be a small hole in the brick. I danced out here and sang. I prayed long and hard until the feeling finally went away. But since I helped you out, I figured I better stay around and enjoy some of that frybread. The smell has been driving me crazy out here!"

The night was filled with joy and laughter. It was as if all the cares of life had fallen away, and the only important thing was to appreciate one another's presence and enjoy the hilarious stories George and Grandmother shared. The children were carried upstairs by Sequoia, Krie and George as yet another pot of tea was brewed. At the top of the stairs, George turned to wink at Sequoia and Krie. He bounded down the stairs, and Krie looked into Sequoia's tired eyes. He reached out and gently moved a stray lock of hair from her face.

"It's not going to be easy for us, Sequoia, but I know that you and I will find our own happiness."

"I know it, too. I know you and I were created for this life. We'll get through it together. And I wouldn't have it any other way."

He leaned forward to kiss her on the cheek. She reached out, caught his face in both hands, and kissed him slowly and deliberately on the mouth. Fire roared from his feet to his scalp. She stood back and smiled. "I feel that too, Krie. We are so blessed." All he could do was nod. How on earth had this beautiful woman come into his life? She grinned widely, knowingly. "I often ask the same about you."

Grandmother was given Sequoia's bed for the night. George took the living room carpet, and Krie the couch.

"I am used to the pavement, and now the floor. Trust me when I tell you that a couch is way too soft for me," George observed.

"Do you want to get set up in a home?" Krie was almost asleep.

"I'll think about it. I am so used to the stars over my head, or the space behind the couch in the Elders' Lounge. I don't know if I could get used to my own place anymore."

◎◎◎

Krie and George and Daniel Delorme were enjoying coffee and eating at the famous Schwartz's Hebrew Delicatessen. Dan was finger painting with his coffee on the red and white paper placemat. The meeting with the Angels had not gone well.

"They laughed *me* out of the clubhouse," Daniel said. The long narrow deli was packed with the midweek lunch crowd and the patrons were loud. There was no worry about being overheard here. Krie's sandwich was so thick, he could barely wrap his jaws around it. He had no idea what Montreal Smoked Meat was, but he loved it. He took alternate sips of Cott Black Cherry soda and coffee in between delicious bites.

"What do you suggest we do?"

Daniel was thoughtful.

"Well, I'd say we start with the Vietnamese, but they'd probably get violent. The South Americans won't consider it. If all else fails, there is the Skynz."

"I thought that gang was long dead." George looked confused.

"That's what they would like you to think. It's the second generation now. They're probably more open-minded than most gangs."

"Open-minded is what we need, if you are getting laughed out of places!"

"Krie, George, I think you two should come with me. Treat it like *Dragons' Den*. Get your pitch ready." George and Krie looked at each other. George grinned.

"This is gonna be good."

☉☉☉

It seemed like a regular business meeting. An Indigenous man sat opposite them at a table. He was dressed in a suit, hair neat in one long braid down his back. They could have been sitting across from Elijah Harper as a young man. They met at the warehouse. The security guy had accepted their case of 24 beer and was off somewhere enjoying it.

"We don't introduce ourselves."

"We have some product we need to move."

"There's no money in cigarettes or pot."

"Uh, noooooo. Maple syrup." Krie was serious.

"You're shittin' me, right?"

"No, we shit you not." George was serious for once.

"Okay, talk."

Krie gave it his best. Outlined the easy security, the plan, and the low risk of being caught with syrup.

"Well, that's a proposition I didn't expect to consider." Their meeting man was thoughtful. "But I know a guy who happens to be an independent syrup broker."

"Syrup broker?" George was grinning again.

"Yeah, a person can move a lot of things in big syrup barrels besides syrup."

George nodded, sagely.

"I will take this back to my associates. I will call you if they are interested in undertaking this little venture."

"I hope to hear good news," Krie said as he firmly shook the meeting man's hand.

"They are going to go for it," George said as they hopped back into the Elders' van.

"What makes you think so?"

"Because they are competing with Hells Angels, and other international groups here. The competition for regular 'business' is pretty deadly."

"I hope you're right. We have to find buyers, and soon." Krie looked to the sky, an off yellow-grey under the streetlights.

"Here comes the snow."

Krie was in his office calculating how many barrels would fit in the Elders' van with the seats removed. He heard nothing until there was a voice in the doorway.

"Well, bro, I have good news."

There was the man from the meeting leaning on the door jamb, smiling, just like any other Friendship Centre client, except most of them didn't wear suits.

"Yes?"

"Can we sit on the couches? Small spaces don't agree with me."

Krie rose and the two of them sat in the Lounge.

"Our organization would like to take you up on your contracting opportunity."

"Well, that's fantastic news."

"Of course, there is considerable risk on our part, you understand."

"We are the ones obtaining and moving the product." Krie was doubtful.

"Well, you understand, there will be the matter of connecting you to the buyers. It's a risk. If something goes wrong, it could lead back to you."

"We're doing all the heavy lifting." Krie was feeling frustrated.

"Well, it's like this," said the smarmy looking meeting man. "Either you give us 75 percent of your profit, or my cousin at the Montreal Police Department is going to hear a good story."

There was a voice from behind the couch.

"Just take it." A tousled, black head rose as George yawned and rubbed his eyes. The meeting man looked around wildly, obviously worried this was a sting.

"Don't worry, bro. You were the guy who wanted a meeting in my bedroom."

"Take it or leave it."

Krie was mulling when George piped up.

"Bro, we'll take it!"

◉◉◉

It was the final run home across the river. Krie was glad. The night trips had been a killer. Daniel and George checked the river edge for a couple of hundred yards, looking for rotten ice. Krie slumped in the driver's seat, exhausted. He opened his eyes and saw George and Daniel coming toward each other from opposite directions. He heard George say, "Looks good to me."

"It'll do," Daniel agreed.

During the crossing, they were all quiet. Krie – the others must be as tired as he was – running without lights through a ghostly landscape, a flat open space of ice, under an eerie blue sky in the inky moonlight.

"We're going have to put all the seats back into the bus, so we don't arouse suspicion in the morning."

"Do we have to?" George was obviously done in.

"Yeah, we …" There was a strange sound. Krie's stomach keeled toward his boots. He knew that sound. Breaking ice!

"Bail!" Krie yelled. "Bail out NOW!" Krie and Daniel made a mad scramble out of the door as the van listed hard to the left and front and the sound of shushing water was heard. Krie turned as he heard the emergency door in the back open and saw George's back as he dove out. There was water around his ankles on the top step and open water below.

"Jump, I'll catch you," Daniel called to Krie.

"Okay, and if I go in, grab me by the jacket, for the love of God."

Krie leapt as high and far as his body would allow. One foot was in water, and by some miracle the ice where he landed held. Daniel hauled him up, and away from the edge of the open water.

Within seconds, the van lowered, nose first, into the black, still water. As the back end rose almost straight up in the air, the lights inside water were visible in the front windows as it filled the inside. There was a sickening sound as the water suffocated the air inside. With a huge "gluck," it was swallowed by the dark water.

"How the hell will we explain this?" Krie's voice was shaking.

"Simple, the van was stolen," Daniel's voice was low. Krie's head was turning in all directions.

"Where's George?"

"Do you see him?"

"Oh my God, you don't think …" Krie couldn't say it.

"He went through the ice?" Daniel finished his thought.

Krie and Daniel looked carefully around for George when they reached the edge of the river. They walked quietly up the boat launch – not speaking, hands in pockets. Daniel lit a smoke.

"Can I have one?"

"You don't smoke."

"I think I do, now!"

"Should we go and look up and down the river further?"

"He'll be alright."

"What if he went in?"

"Then there's nothing we can do."

"I don't want to think of that possibility.

"Neither do I."

They walked the rest of the way in total silence.

Sequoia was pale when Krie dragged himself into the Friendship Centre.

"Krie, I heard on the news that a big hole was found in the middle of the river this morning by a speed skater. Are you alright?"

"Well, no. We are out one van, and one George. His eyes filled with tears.

"Come into my office," and she pulled him by the hand.

"Oh my God, Krie, what happened?"

"The van went through the ice, and we couldn't find George!"

Her face went a shade paler, and she bit her lip. Her eyes streamed tears, and she took him in her arms. She could feel the silent sobs, his body shaking like the last clinging, dry leaves in a fall gust.

"Krie, we have to hold hope, we have to."

"Oh my God, I am never going to be able to forgive myself."

"It wasn't your fault!"

"I feel responsible. And why did Daniel and I get out of it, and not George? I feel like I failed him." Sequoia stepped back, held his face in her hands.

"Krie, he would have no regrets; I have never seen him more alive, happier, than when you were all involved in this thing."

"That might be true, but he's not alive now."

◉◉◉

Later that day, Sequoia came into the Elders' Lounge where Krie was slumped at his desk staring into space.

"Someone was found, Krie, down by the river. I don't know if it's George, but they described him as a First Nations male in his mid-30s. I think one of us should offer to identify him."

He had never been in a morgue. They went together. He insisted on going in alone. Once the forms had been signed, he was taken by the officer and attendant to a room where a small sheet-covered the body. Krie's heart was in his throat. The attendant waited for his signal, and Krie took a deep breath. The attendant peeled back the sheet.

"It's not him." Krie's voice was quiet.

"Can I have a moment, for cultural reasons?" The cop had a quizzical look, but the attendant nodded and respectfully left the room. Krie prayed over the body. He finished with: "I may not know who you are, but you were someone's child, someone's family. Go well, brother."

Sequoia looked up. He shook his head, no, and she let out a big breath, and bowed her head.

"I mean no disrespect but thank God!" Krie nodded, and they walked out into the cold.

◉⊚◉

There was a knock at Krie's bedroom door. He groaned, rolled over, and croaked out a "Yes." It was his first full night of sleep in a couple of months, and he was sick from exhaustion.

"Krie, the phone. It's Yukon calling." Mme. Brodeur sounded urgent.

"Hello?"

"Krie?"

"Haywire! Holy cow, it's so good to hear your voice!"

"You too, Krie, I'm sorry, but I have bad news."

"Oh no! What is it, are you okay?"

"Yes, but Uncle ... He's gone Krie."

"No. I wasn't there ... I ..."

"Krie, it's okay. He got me to write you a letter, just yesterday. I'm going to send it. He must have known. He told me to say in it that no matter what happens, you have to stay in Quebec for the year like you planned, right to the end, before you come home."

"But I want to come home."

"Krie, it's best you don't. Honour Uncle's wishes, and your mother will be here, anyways. It may break her to see you. She'd recognize you. She seems to be doing better, but she's not all the way, okay. Wait 'til the one-year memorial. Uncle would want you to stay, follow through. He knew you had kids to take care of. Your job and other commitments. He wanted you to see it all through."

"It's going to hurt like hell to know he isn't going to be there to greet me when I come home." Krie's voice cracked.

"Yes, he will, just like he is with you right now. He was proud of you, Krie, he talked about you all the time. He loved you like his own. Just keep being who you are. Keep to your plan and come home in the summer. I will be here. You and I can design his headstone for the memorial together, okay?"

"Haywire, are you gonna be okay?" Krie was bereft.

"I will be. And I get to see your Mom soon, and you know that will make things alright for me."

"I know it will, and I am glad," Krie was overwhelmed for a moment.

"When I come home, I'm never leaving again. There's nothing anywhere else for me."

"Well, it will be good to have you home again, that's for sure."

"When you hug my Mother, think of me."

Haywire's voice broke. "I will, Krie, I will. And Krie?"

"Yeah, Haywire?"

"I'm proud of you, too. And I hope my sons grow up to be just like you."

Uncle's letter arrived a few days later, by courier. Krie didn't read it at first but put it on his bedside table. It wasn't time. He'd planned a pipe ceremony for Uncle tonight because he knew the family ceremony would be going on at the same time.

Sequoia, her Grandmother, Mme. Brodeur, the children, and Gladys all sat around the blanket. Krie placed Uncle's letter on the altar. They sat within the sweet fragrance of the medicine smoke and prayed together.

At the end, Krie opened the letter and began to read aloud.

Dear Krie

Arthur is writing for me. Boy, me, I have been thinking of you. Every day. Miss telling you "wanna fight?" Sure, hope that you know that I am proud of you. All the good things you are doing. I am proud that you went from a hard time to the man you are now. We are all proud of you. I know your time there is not what you thought. It's what it's s'posed to be. Just like when we trapped; never knew what we would find when we walked the line. One day a good fur, and the next, a ruined one. It's how life is. You are a good man and will always find your way. I wish I had more time with you. It did me good to have you here. It gave me someone to teach. I never had a son, but I would like him to be like you. A friend of yours showed up here. George, [there were gasps all around the blanket … Krie looked up, face glowing with wonder, and then went back to reading.] *He's from Inuvik. He was on his way home but wanted you to know he said hi. He told us some good stories about all you guys did. Told us he thought he'd knew he better skedaddle home right away after what happened. He'll send his address once he's home. He smiles a lot. He sure thinks the world of you. Anyways, I want you to know you have made me happy and proud. Keep on you path. Come home when it's all done. And I will say hello to your Grandmother for you.*

Love always,
Uncle Angus

"My God, George is alive." Gladys was exultant.

"Can you believe it?" Sequoia laughed.

"Thanks, God," Mme. Brodeur was holding her chest.

"Goodbye, Uncle, travel well," Krie said quietly.

◉◎◉

The Elders were huddled together and speaking in low tones, but the energy in the room was high.

"I am so angry at this news article about the heist."

"Why? Nobody figured us out – just mentioned weird marks in the snow as a clue."

"Walker and cane tracks," Gladys snorted. "It's not rocket science!"

"Well, the main thing is the heat's off and the police are dropping the investigation." Krie was philosophical.

"*Vermont maple sugar candy producer alleged to have been caught with 12 trucks worth of undocumented syrup. Police were unable to trace it back to the $20-million theft of the golden elixir from a central warehouse outside of Montreal.*"

"Hah"! So now the syrup Cartel is cashing in on the insurance." Ned chortled.

"I guess there are criminals everywhere." Gladys threw the paper down.

"Still, that was a nice van," Ellie sighed.

"Well, we will get another, and we will ensure it is just as good, maybe better! Meantime, you are set to plan your casino trip."

"What are we going to do for a van?" Sadie was grumpy looking.

"Insurance," Krie said. "But the paperwork could take some time."

"What about the evidence cited in the news article?" Ned's jaw was tight, and his eyes steady.

"There are a lot of walkers and wheelchairs in Quebec. Anyone could have left those tracks outside the warehouse." Krie tried to make his voice sound soothing.

"I don't like that the reporter made a joke about the Fogie Gang. That's disrespectful," complained Gladys. "We'll just have to rent a van, because we have planned our trip, and we want to leave within two weeks!"

"There is one thing I need to let you know." Krie paused; the words did not want to let themselves out.

"Daniel Delorme will be driving and escorting you; he got hired as the replacement Elders' Coordinator."

"Why are we in need of a replacement?"

"In four weeks, I am going home to the North. I lost my Uncle, and I am being called. The land and mountains are speaking to me, calling me back. I feel what I came here to do is done. My Uncle said to stay until I knew it was time. It's time."

Silence fell like snow far in the Northern forest.

◉◉◉

It was time. Krie and Haywire were sanding the carved wooden headstone.

"I think Uncle will love the design on here."

"It was a good idea, Krie. I knew he would want a natural picture, but it was a great idea to give him the view from the window of the cabin."

"It isn't perfect, but I think he will like this."

"I know he will."

"I guess that's it." Haywire put down the sanding block. "Where's that linseed oil?"

"I warmed it on top of the stove while I brewed coffee."

"After we're done." Haywire hesitated, "I told the cooks I would be dropping the maple syrup off at the gym for the give-away. I'll meet you at the graveyard. This is Carcross. People aren't going to be there right on time, remember."

"Yeah, that's right. Still on city time. I forgot about those ancient rhythms."

"Ancient rhythms?"

"Yeah, you know, how everyone just has a sense, collectively, when something should start?"

"Collectively? You talk like your Mom."

"Yeah. Like whoever wants to be there is there, and everyone there feels it. It's funny, that."

"Okay, see you down there, I want to give myself plenty of time to unload the truck without breaking into a big sweat."

"Are you expecting someone there that you are worried about how you look?"

Haywire flashed him a grin, "You!"

"No, that someone is in Quebec and isn't ready to leave her homeland. Sequoia's Grandmother is there, her whole family is there, and her life is there."

"I know, it's just hard to see you mooning around."

"I'll learn to live with it," he said. "You did, Uncle did."

"Yup, true, we did, and you will, too. That lonesome feeling will never leave. It's best if you make friends with it. It's not going *anywhere*."

Krie breathed deeply all the way to Whitehorse. The plan was that he was now going to pick up his Mother. She could react in some way he wasn't expecting, and he had to be ready for anything. This was hard. How was he going to keep it cool and still try to get to know her and create a bond, at the same time?

He waited in the crowd, a little distant from the rest around the luggage carousel. What if he didn't recognize her? What if he didn't even see her in this mob? Thoughts whirled, and he started the breathing, in four, hold seven, out eight. And then, there she was, standing tall and beautiful like a willow in the meadow. Mother. As if she knew he was there, her luggage beside her. Like a deer in the wild, her head swung up, searching. Her eyes locked on his; her face went pale. He held his breath. She crumpled to the ground.

Krie rushed to her, his heart pounding, and cradled her head in his lap. She stirred and opened her eyes.

"Hello, I am Krie," he said gently, before fear could enter her shining black eyes. "I am Haywire's foster son. I'm back from Montreal." He was waiting for her to speak. She didn't. She looked at him, long and hard. Her voice was weak. "I didn't know of you; you look exactly like someone I knew once, but I can't recall who." He sees the tears and feels her trembling from head to toe. He smiles, hoping it will calm her.

"Are you feeling alright now?" He gave her a little water from a bottle in his hand. She sat up, others moved away now, it was just the two of them. Colour had come back into her face, and she was no longer shaking.

"Who's your Father?" Stricken, he did not know how to answer her.

"He died."

"I'm really sorry to stare, but you look exactly like someone I know; but it's weird, I don't remember."

"That's okay I get that a lot." He felt tears well up but did not want to disturb her again. He laughed instead.

"I was fostered out before I was born. I just know my Dad never knew about me."

"So, how is it that you came North?

"Has it been what you were looking for?"

"It has, and it hasn't – what I know has only made me know I know nothing." She laughs at this.

"Yes, I think we all know that feeling." Krie felt deeply concerned.

"Do you think you're feeling okay enough to stand?"

"I think so – I'm so sorry; this is so embarrassing."

"Just hold on to me." She leaned heavily on him to get up on shaky legs. He was gentle with her. She felt so frail, like an egg that could crack or a newborn animal trying to stand for the first time. He let her lean as she swayed a little.

"Take your time; you look like you need a few minutes; do you need to sit?" He felt strangely at peace with this woman who was his Mother; deeply rooted in the earth like a tree.

"I am fine, honestly. I think I just need to get out of here!"

"Let me get your bags," Krie said. "Cousin Lorna asked me to come and get you."

She continued looking at him without speaking.

"Krie, forgive me for staring," she said, filling her eyes with him. He smiled a knowing smile but said nothing.

◉◉◉

Leah was enjoying the clean energy of this young man, Krie. He felt like a fire on a cold day by which she could warm herself. She was curious.

"Krie, did you grow up traditional?"

He was careful. "I did, and I didn't. My foster Mother was my Auntie as it turns out. Long story. I found that out when my Grandmother showed up in my life. My Mother's Mother. Up until then, I grew up urban in the South."

"I can tell you are connected to culture. Who had such an influence on you?"

"My Grandmother, and then later Haywire and Gramma Maisey and Uncle Angus. It was like I was a dead cell phone plugging myself into Tlingit-Tagish culture and recharging."

"Ah. And have you learned anything of your Father?"

"I still know nothing of my Father, still because people will not share stories. I know a lot about him by the way people *don't* answer questions about him and the expressions on people's faces. Without words, these people have shared the dark, the light."

He could sense that Leah was relaxed, deeply peaceful. That it was the first time in a long time. She was easy to be with. Uncharacteristically, he talked all the way to Little Annie. She listened, smiling. They reached the road to the cabin. Leah put a hand on his arm.

"Please stop a minute." Outside of the truck, she stood and took some deep breaths. When she got back in, she smiled at him.

"I wanted to taste the exhaled breath of the trees."

"I did that after I'd been in Montreal for a year." They bumped and rattled down the old road, and he was careful with the truck. The cabin came into view, and he parked on the wild chamomile grass in front. The placid, deep blue lake reflected the clear sky. There was no sound. He looked at Leah.

"It's kinda nice to be with someone who knows about being city and country."

"Likewise, and you saved me a teasing from somebody country accusing me of needing to shake off the coffee high."

He laughed; hopped out to unload.

He chopped wood as she settled in. She took the water pail out and hauled water from the creek. She looked as though she was struggling, so he ran to help her across the last bit and into the cabin.

He was like the fragrance of this land. Like the sunrise, and the promise of a new day. When he brought the last load of wood and asked if there was anything else she needed, Leah had this feeling that she was going miss his presence and wanted him to stay. She shook it off. She listened to the truck engine fading. Part of him was still here.

Krie took the road from the cabin with tears streaming down his face. When he reached the top of the road, he stopped the truck, broke down, and sobbed like a small boy.

☺☺☺

Krie was spent. Weakness left his body trembling. He felt like a child. Nausea rose, and he willed it down. He made his way to a creek and drank, deep and long. He lay on the moss, listening to its voice as it ran by him toward Annie Lake. It was like his heart and his blood, which he thought would always flow toward the lake. He breathed the scent of the moss, the bush tea, the earth, the trees, the exhaled breath of this land so precious to his heart. He lay knowing the sense of all of these, and the ancient earth below him satiating his exhaustion. He rolled over and looked at the sky. That big, clear sky that only here spoke to him with its own deep blue. Clouds sailed on the blue like swans across the still in the fall lake. He felt the earth beneath him, holding his weight. He felt the deep silence and heard the enormity of it. An eagle soared above the meadows – high – and his heart rose, soaring with it. They had done it. Mother was safe. He hoisted himself to his elbow and saw Haywire with Mother, coming toward him. Tears came and ran down his cheeks as he saw them make their way to him. He stood, waiting for them. When they were close enough, Mother stopped, and stared at him, holding her hands to her heart. He could see tears flowing down her cheeks. He waited. It was the same sense as when he wanted to will a wild animal to approach him.

"Mother" was all he could say. Haywire stood with them, but apart. He had that gentle smile of his when Krie met his eyes. Krie held his Mother until she pulled back.

"I'm sorry I wasn't strong enough to know you." Her voice was redolent with heartbreak.

"But you are now," Krie said with all the love that he could.

"I understand now, why I had to suffer so much."

"Why, Mother?"

"Because you are who you are. I am grateful for all I went through, because you came from it. I will thank Creator until the end of my days for all my trials. There is such beauty in it, Krie, such meaning in it all. It owned me for so long, broke me in two, and now it is fusing me together.

"Life is the greatest mystery. We can never truly know why things happen. I only know it is a great gift when we rarely get to see why things happened the way they did.

"My son. My son. My Krie. My sweet boy. I never want to let you go."

"You will never have to, Mother." Speaking that word opened something within him. It was as if a tight bud deep within his heart opened like a wild rose, petal by petal. His entire being was filled with it.

"We have always had each other, Mother. Always. And we always will."

They held each other for what seemed like a very long time before she finally stood back. They couldn't take their eyes off one another.

"I feel whole. For the first time, I know what it is to be whole." Krie's voice sounded childlike to his ears.

It was then that he felt an overpowering spirit from between the trees across the meadow. He knew she would come to him. One day. His heartbeat became one hard, leaping beat and it sang her name.

"Sequoia!"

ACKNOWLEDGEMENTS

I have much gratitude for all who made this book possible.

To Stands in the Middle who is an ally in all I do, who loves me unconditionally, and graces all my days with generosity of spirit, kindness, and best of all, laughter.

For my Matriarchs who saw me, believed in me, even when I didn't believe in myself. My adoptive Mom the late Katherine (Kitty) Grant (nee Smarch), my late bio-Mother, Joan (Cole) (White) (Playfair). And so many others who are dancing among the stars.

To the Dak`laweidí Wolf Clan who I am proud to stand and live with.

For Linda Rogers, Warrior Woman and Universal Mother who stands for every human and inspires us with her lived poetry. To her partner Rick Van Krugel for being as delightfully you and funny as I need you to be. Thanks for being the best arty friends and allies of all time.

To Aliya Grant, who at 12, decided that I must trap the Bonewalker *inside* the house, and changed the story forever. Love you my girl.

To the Callaghan Clan who embody integrity and genius, thanks for including me in wolf pack of exiles and other misfits. You who apparently swore a blood oath to accept, love, protect, and fight for us to the death. Deeply grateful to be among you.

To Exile Editions for providing stellar literature to the masses.

To the entire extended Exile Family, a carefully curated delightful rabble of quiet (and not so quiet) rebels who shine like the stars above.

To Daniel David Moses who vaulted me into a new sphere as a Writer and who is now among the Star People. I miss you.

To Lee Maracle who pretty much told me I was publishing, and who showed her pride generously. I can hear you laughing from the stars.

To the entire Smarch-Grant family who took me as one of their own. You are treasured.

To Thunder Elk who I miss each day. Need coffee and smokes, *don't* you?

For Mark Preston, who designed the lush artwork for the book cover. Hope you're enjoying the stars. You will always be missed. All I see when I think of you is that grin.

For my sister, Leslie Gentile, who listens and shares all things "writing."

To Marsha Boulton who had her hawk eyes on this work, and who puts her heart into it all.

To Randall Perry and all others who had eyes on this work. I am deeply grateful.

Karen Lee White is Salish, Tuscarora, Chippewa, and Scots who lives in the territory of the lək^wəŋən and Xwsepsum People (Vancouver Island, British Columbia). Karen was adopted by the Dak`laweidí Wolf Clan of the Interior Tlingit-Tagish people on whose land her second novel *Bonewalker* unfolds.

The Silence, her first novel – which includes a CD of the author's original music – was released in 2018, and went into a second printing after just six weeks.

In 2018 the Banff Centre commissioned a short story for their large box set *Fables of the 21st Century* (a limited edition for gala fundraising), and in 2017 Karen was awarded an Indigenous Art Award for Writing by the Hnatyshyn Foundation. Her work has appeared in the anthologies *Impact: Colonialism in Canada, That Damned Beaver, Bawaajigan,* and *Mother,* as well as the periodicals *Verb, EXILE, alive,* among others.

She is also a playwright, and has been commissioned by theatres in Vancouver and Victoria.